Acclaim 1

At the

JIM BRIDGER

Stories

Ron Carlson

PICADOR
NEW YORK

www.picadorusa.com

For information on Picador Reading Group Guides, as well as ordering, please contact the Trade Marketing department at St. Martin's Press.
Phone: 1-800-221-7945 extension 763
Fax: 212-677-7456
E-mail: trademarketing@stmartins.com

"Towel Season," "At the Jim Bridger," and "The Potato Gun" appeared in *Esquire*; "The Clicker at Tips," "Evil Eye Allen," and "At the El Sol" appeared in *Tin House*; "Disclaimer" and "Single Woman for Long Walks on the Beach" appeared in *Harper's*; "The Ordinary Son" appeared in *The Oxford American*; "At Copper View" appeared in *Five Points*; "Garry Garrison's Wedding Vows" appeared in *Glimmer Train*.

Additionally: "Towel Season" appears in *The Big Esquire Book of Fiction and Symphony Space Selected Shorts Audio Vol. XIV*; "At the Jim Bridger" and "At Copper View" appear in *The O. Henry Prize Stories 2001*; "The Ordinary Son" appears in *The Best American Short Stories 2000* and *The Pushcart Prize Anthology 2001*; "Disclaimer" appeared in *Witness* and *The Human Project*; "Single Woman for Long Walks on the Beach" appeared in *The Hawaii Review*.

Library of Congress Cataloging-in-Publication Data

Carlson, Ron.
    At the Jim Bridger : stories / Ron Carlson.
      p. cm.
    ISBN 0-312-28605-8 (hc)
    ISBN 0-312-30724-1 (pbk)
  1. United States—Social life and customs—20th Century—Fiction. I. Title.

PS3553.A733 A92 2002
813'.54—dc21   2001059065

First Picador Paperback Edition: May 2003

D10 9 8 7 6 5 4 3

For Elaine

CONTENTS

I

Towel Season 3

At the Jim Bridger 19

The Clicker at Tips 43

Disclaimer 55

II

The Ordinary Son 61

Evil Eye Allen 85

At Copper View 105

Single Woman for Long Walks on the Beach 125

III

The Potato Gun 131

Gary Garrison's Wedding Vows 153

At the El Sol 169

I

TOWEL SEASON

SUDDENLY IT WAS JUNE AND there were strange towels in the
house. There were stacks on the table in the entry, two or three
towels that Edison knew were not their towels. In the hall, he'd
step over large striped piles of strange wet towels waiting to be
washed. The kids, Rebecca and Toby, pedaled home in bathing
suits, alien towels hung on their necks. Twice Edison tripped as
he sidled through the laundry room carrying his files, his feet
tangled in a great heap of these damp things. The commotion
brought Leslie from the kitchen and she looked down at him,
the absentminded professor, his papers around his head.
"You're kind of too young for this kind of thing," she said. He
didn't look uncomfortable. She knew if she left him there and
went back to her potato salad, there was a good chance he'd
simply go to sleep. He was up past one almost every night
working on his largest mathematical project. This was his final
experimental journey for the firm; if it worked, he was going to
be able to go on and on toward the edge. If not, he would join
all the other middle-level engineers.

"Whose towels are these?"

The answer was, depending on the day, the Hanovers', the
Plums', the Reeds'; close-radius towels, the Hanovers and
their pool just down the street, the Plums and their pool
around the corner, and the Reeds and their pool not three

blocks across from the elementary school all the children (nine total) of these people attended.

"These, dear, are the Plums' and we'll be returning them this evening when we go over there for a cookout, so get your work done." She picked up his files and laid them on his chest. "Okay? Swimming? Drinks on their patio? Remember? Don't worry, when the time comes, I'll drive us all over."

Edison crawled to his feet. "All right." Leslie watched him go into his study, and then she stuffed the towels in the washer. He was working on the most advanced and important calculations of his life. The firm only kept one or two theoretical mathematicians, and this project would determine if Edison would make the cut.

The summer developed into these dinners and all the shifting towels. That night, they loaded the car and drove five hundred yards to the Plums' and drifted with the Hanovers and the Reeds toward the gate, carrying their coolers and casseroles and Tupperware containers and the bundle of towels. They seemed like zombies in a fog to Edison, because he was in a fog most of the time himself, so many hours working at his computer screen, and inside the greetings continued even though they'd all seen one another at the Reeds' three nights ago. Edison and Allen Reed opened bottles of Corona and sat out on the picnic table in the steady heat of the season. These outings always disoriented Edison, who saw them as some kind of puzzle. Part of him was still at his green screen mulling equations while he watched the children spill into the green pool and the women set out the food.

"How's the project going, Ed?" Allen asked him. Allen Reed, large and tan, was an applications engineer for the firm. Ed looked at the man's skin, so dark from the sun he seemed part of the strangeness. What kind of engineer has such a tan? Allen was about five years older than Edison and had an affectionate condescension for theoretical math.

"I'm working every day," Edison said. He was looking at the bench where all the towels had gathered in stacks: fourteen towels. There was no way those towels were going home with the right families. Folded there in multicolored order, they seemed part of some problem Edison had solved this week or dreamed of or was working on now.

"Yes, well, you let me know when they find a market for chaos and its theory, and I'll come over with my slide rule and give you a hand." Allen was going to pat Edison on the shoulder, which he did with people he was kidding, but he saw that Edison was about two seconds from getting the joke. They were all used to these odd moments with Edison.

The thing that was said about Edison at least once every party, after he'd been asked a question and then waited five or ten seconds to answer, or after one of his rare remarks, was "I'm glad I'm not a genius," which was meant as a kind of compliment and many times simply as a space filler after some awkwardness.

And even early in the summer on the way home from a cookout, Toby, who was six years old, started crying and when questioned about his grief, stuttered out in a whisper, "Daddy's a genius!" He cried as Leslie carried him to the house in one of the large pale blue towels that Edison knew was not their towel, and he cried himself to sleep.

Undressing for bed, Leslie said, "Ed, can you lighten up a little, fit in? These are my friends."

"Sure," he said as she got in bed beside him. "I think I can do that." A long moment later, he turned to Leslie and said, "But I'm not a genius. I'm just in a tough section of this deal now. Can you tell Toby? I'm just busy. I need to finish this project."

"I know you do," she whispered. "What should I tell him it's like?" When they were dating, he'd begun to try to explain his work to her in metaphors, and she'd continued the game through his career, asking him for comparisons that then she'd inhabit, embellish. Right after they were married and Edison was in graduate school, he'd work late into the night in their apartment and crawl into bed with the calculations still percolating in his head. "What's it like?" Leslie would ask. "Where are you now?" She could tell he was remote, lit. They talked in territories.

"I've crossed all the open ground and the wind has stopped now. My hope is to find a way through this next place."

"Mountains?"

"Right. Okay, mountains, blank, very few markings." He spoke carefully and with a quiet zeal. "They're steep, hard to see."

"Is it cold?"

"No, but it is strange. It's quiet." Then he'd turn to her in bed, his eyes bright, alive. "I'm way past the path. I don't think anyone has climbed this route before. There are no trails, handholds."

Leslie would smile and kiss him in that close proximity. "Keep going," she'd say. "Halfway up that mountain, there's a woman with a cappuccino cart and a chicken salad sandwich: me."

Then a smile would break across his face, too, and he would see her, kiss her back, and say it: "Right. You."

Now in bed, Edison said, "Tell him it's like . . ." He paused and ran the options. "Playing hide-and-seek."

"At night. In the forest?"

"Yes." He was whispering. "It's a forest and parts of this thing are all over the place. It's going to take a while."

The Hanovers' party was like all the parties, a ritual that Edison knew well. The kids swam while the adults drank, then the kids ate and went off into the various corners of the house primarily for television, and then the adults ate their grilled steaks or salmon or shish kebabs and drank a new wine while it got dark and they flirted. It was easy and harmless and whoever was up was sent to the kitchen or the cooler for more potato salad or beer and returned and gave whatever man or woman whatever he or she had asked for and said as a husband or wife might, "There you are, honey. Can I get you anything else, dear?" And maybe there'd be some nudging, a woman punctuating the sentence with her hip at a man's shoulder or a man taking a woman's shoulders in both hands possessively.

At some point there'd be Janny Hanover and Scott Plum coming out of the house holding hands and Janny announcing, "Scott and I have decided to elope," and he'd add, "I've got to have a woman who uses mayonnaise on everything." In their swimsuits in the dark, arms around each waist, now parting and rejoining the group, they did look as if it were a possibility. The eight adults were interchangeable like that, as swimsuit silhouettes, Edison thought, except me, I'm too skinny and too tall, I'd look like a woman's father walking out of the patio doors like that. I'd scare everybody. Around the pool, the towels glowed in random splashes where they'd been thrown. Edison listened to the men and women talk, and when they laughed, he tried to laugh, too.

Days, while Leslie took Toby and Becky to the shoe store, the orthodontist, tennis lessons, Edison worked on his project. He was deep in the fields, each problem more like a long, long hike. He had to go way into each to see the next corner and then there to see forward. He had to keep his mind against it the entire time; one slip and he'd have to backtrack. Edison described his work to Leslie now the same way he began to think of it, as following little people through the forest: some would weave through the trees, while others would hide behind trees and change clothes, emerging at a different speed. He had to keep track of all of them, shepherd them through the trees and over a hill that was not quite yet in

sight and line them up for a silver bus. The silver bus was
Leslie's contribution. He'd work on butcher paper with pencils, and then after two or three o'clock, he would enter his
equations into the computer and walk out into his house, his
face vague, dizzy, not quite there yet.

Summer began in earnest and women began stopping by
with towels. Edison would hear Janny Hanover or Paula
Plum call from the front hall, the strange female voices coming to him at first from the field of numbers progressing
across the wide paper. "Don't get up! It's just me! See you
tonight at the Reeds'!" and then the door would shut again
and Edison would fight with his rising mind to stay close to
the shifting numerals as they squirmed and wandered. He
felt, at such moments, as if he were trying to gather a para-
chute in a tricky and persistent wind.

Some days there'd be a tan face suddenly at his study door,
Paula Plum or Melissa Reed, saying, "So this is where the
genius does it," and placing two or three folded towels on the
chair. The incursion was always more than Edison could
process. He looked up at the woman, a hot-pink tank top, sunglasses in her hair, and felt as if he'd been struck. The calcu-
lation bled, toppled. Edison felt involved in some accident, his
hands collapsed, his heartbeat in his face. Then she was gone,
whoever she had been, singing something about tonight or
tomorrow night at the Plums' or the Reeds', and Edison found
himself dislocated, wrecked. His children knew not to barge
in that way, because it meant his day's work vanished, and
he'd spend hours looking out the front window or walking the
neighborhood in the summer heat. The chasm between his
pencil figurings and the figures of the real world was that, a
chasm, and there was no bridge.

At the Reeds' and the Plums' while the kids splashed in the
pool and Scott flirted with Melissa and Allen with Paula, sil-

houettes passing in and out of the house as summer darkness finally fell while everyone was fed grilled meat of all kinds and Paula Plum's tart potato salad, word got out that Edison was *brusque*, at least not hospitable, and Janny Hanover lifted her wine to him, saying, "Why, darling, you looked absolutely like I was going to steal your trigonometry!" Edison smiled at her, feeling Leslie's gaze; he promised he'd try to do better. Holding this smile was pure effort.

"And you looked at me like you didn't even know who I was," Paula added.

Edison didn't know what to say, held the smile, tried to chuckle, might have, and then it became painfully clear that he should say something. He couldn't say what he thought: I don't know who you are. The faces glowed in a circle around him, the healthy skin, all those white teeth. "Well, my heavens," and there was a pause which they all knew they would fall into, and people knew they would have to do something—cough, get up for more beer, make a joke. He'd done this to this group a dozen times already this summer, what an oddball. Then he spoke: "Do you ladies go through the neighborhood surprising every geek who's double-checking his lottery numbers?"

And the pause sparked and Dan Hanover laughed, roared, and the laughter carried all of them across, and it was filled with gratitude and something else that Edison saw in Leslie's eyes, something about him: he'd scored a point. There was a new conviviality through the night, more laughter, the men brought Edison another beer, Leslie suddenly at ease. Children drifted in and out of the pool, docking between their parents' legs for a moment, then floated away, dropping towels here and there. Edison, the new center of the group, felt strange: warm and doomed.

The following days were different than any he'd known. People treated him, how? Cordially, warmly, more than that.

This new fellowship confused him. He'd obviously broken the code and was inside now. His research crashed and vanished. At the butcher paper with his pencils he was like a man in the silent woods at night, reaching awkwardly for things he could not see. "I'm going in circles."

"Is any of it familiar? Is there a moon?" Leslie asked. "Shall I honk the horn of the silver bus? Start a bonfire?"

"There's no light, no wind. I'm stalled."

"Go uphill. You'll see the horizon."

But he didn't. The work he'd done, all the linkages had been delicate, and after two days the numbers paled and dried and the adhesive dissipated, and while he stared at the sheet, the ragged edge of the last figures, it all ran away. He was going to have to turn around, follow the abstruse calculations back until he could gather it all again. Edison left the room. He walked the long blocks of his neighborhood in the heat, lost and stewing.

Days, he began to ferry the kids around and was surprised to start learning the names of their friends, the young Plums, the Hanover girl, the Reed twins. He was surprised by everything, the pieces of a day, the way they fit and then fled. He'd wait in the van at the right hour, and the children would wander out of the movie theater and climb in. It was a wonder. He started cooking, which he'd always enjoyed, but now he started cooking all the time. Permutations on grilled cheese sandwiches, variations on spaghetti.

He delivered towels, returning stacks of cartoon characters to the Hanovers, Denver Bronco logo towels to the Plums, who had moved here from Colorado, and huge striped things to the Reeds, always trading for his family's mongrel assemblage. He became familiar with the women, dropping in on them at all daytime hours, calling in the front doors, "Man in the house," and hearing after a beat, Janny or Melissa or

Paula call, "Thank heaven for that, come on in." If the kids were in the car, he'd drop the towels and greetings and hurry out; if not, sometimes it was coffee. Melissa Reed put a dollop of Jägermeister in hers; Janny Hanover drank directly out of a liter Evian bottle, offering him any of her husband's ales (Dan was a member of Ale of the Month); Paula made him help her make lemonade from scratch. All of the women were grateful for the company. These visits and the weekend parties made Edison in his new life feel as if he were part of a new, larger family, with women and children everywhere; he was with people more than he'd ever been in his life.

In bed he didn't want to talk; his hands ran over Leslie in his approach. She held him firmly, adjusted, asked, "What is it like now, the project?" Edison put his head against her neck, stopped still for a beat, and then began again working along her throat. "Ed, should I worry about you? Where are you with the research?" He lifted away from her in the dark, and then his hand descended and she caught it. She turned toward him now and he pulled to free his hand, but she held it. It was an odd moment for them. "Edison," she said. "What is going on?" They were lying still, not moving. "Are you okay? Have you stumbled on a log and hit your head on a sharp outcropping? Has a mighty bear chased you up a nasty tree? Did he bite you? Should I call that helicopter they use in the mountains?" He could hear the smile in her voice. "What do you need me to do? Where are the little people?" It was clear he was not going to answer. "They're waiting for you. Go get them. And I'm waiting, too, remember? By the silver bus. You'll make it, Ed." But when she let go of his hand and kissed him, he held still one second and then simply turned away.

The project needed to be done this season; it couldn't smolder for another year. They'd take him off it, and have him counting beans in the group cubicles. They put you out on the frontier like this once, and when you came back beaten, you joined one of the teams, your career in close orbit, the adventure gone.

Meanwhile, he fled the house. He'd stand close to Paula at the counter while they squeezed the lemons, their arms touching; he began having a drop of Jäger with Melissa, and when Janny Hanover would see him to the door, they'd hug for five seconds, which is one second over the line. He could feel her water bottle against his back.

Some afternoons Leslie would stand in the doorway of his little study and see the spill of pencils where they'd been for days. She kept the hallway clear of laundry, but he never went to that corner of the house anymore. They circled each other through the days. In bed he was silent. She tried to open him. "Okay, mister, should I try to drive the bus closer, honk the horn? You want me to bring in some of those all-terrain vehicles? Some kind of signal? We're running low on crackers."

After a moment, he said, "I'm not sure."

"Can you see any landmarks, stars?"

"Not really," he answered. "I can't." His voice was flat, exhausted, as he tried to imagine it all. "It's steep. It's too dark. I'm having some trouble with my footing."

"I know you are. Everybody does," Leslie said, opening her eyes and looking at his serious face. "Keep your own path. Dig your feet in. Try."

Paula wanted to know if he really worked for the CIA; Janny wanted to know if his I.Q. was really two hundred; Melissa asked him if she should get implants. She was drinking her green coffee at the kitchen table and she simply lifted her shirt. The fresh folded towels stood on the corner of the table. The afternoons he was home between errands were the worst. Now his calculations seemed a cruel puzzle, someone else's work, dead, forgotten, useless.

Edison was a light at the parties, sharing recipes and inside information on the children. There was always someone at his right hand talking, a man or a woman; he was open now yet still exotic. His difference was clear: he was the only man still not settled, the only man still *becoming*, unknown, and it gave him an allure that Leslie felt, and she watched him the way you watch the beast in a fairy tale, to see if it is really something very good in other clothing. Certainly, the parties were less of a strain for her now, not having to worry about Edison's oddness, his potential for gaffs, but his new state strained everything else.

By August the women's familiarity with Edison was apparent. At the cookouts, they spoke in a kind of shorthand, and others had to ask them to back up, explain, if they were to understand at all. Janny Hanover let her hand drift to Edison's shoulder as they talked. Paula Plum began using certain words she'd learned from him: *vector, valence, viable.* Melissa Reed returned from a week-long trip (supposedly to see her parents in Boulder) with four new swimsuits and a remarkable bustline.

Then suddenly it was Labor Day, an afternoon no different from the hundred before it, but as Edison swept the pool patio and washed the deck chairs and cleaned the grill, he knew summer was, in some way, over. But he wanted the exercise there in his yard, the broom, the hose, the bucket of suds, the sun a steady pressure, and as he wiped the tables and squared the furniture, he thought, No wonder Scott and Dan and Allen like this. The pool was clean, a diamond blue, and there wasn't a crumb on the deck. Edison wandered around another half hour and then he put his tools away with great care.

That evening the women did a slow dance around him. He felt it as confused push and pull; he watched the children in the pool, their groupings and regroupings, and then he'd have a new cold beer in his hand, talking again to Scott Plum about chlorine. He sat in the circle of his friends on folding chairs in the reflected swimming pool light, with Paula or Janny right behind him, hip against his shoulder, and he held everyone's attention now, describing with his hands out in the air a game he'd designed to let the children choose who got to ride in the front seat. "It's called First Thumb," he said, lifting his thumbs from each fist; one, then the other. Edison named the different children and how they played the game, and who had gotten to sit in the front seat today and how. His hands worked liked two puppets. The women laughed, the men smiled, and Janny pulled Edison's empty beer bottle out of his hands and replaced it with a full one.

"You're too much," Dan Hanover said. "This is a hell of a summer for you. I'll be glad when you get this spec project done and get over and give us a hand in applications." He leaned forward and made his hands into a ring, fingertip to fingertip. "We've got engine housings—"

"Not just the housings, the whole acceptor," Allen Reed interrupted. "And the radial displacement and timing has a huge window, anything we want. We've got carte blanche, Ed."

"*Fund*-ing! You'd be good on this team," Dan Hanover said.

"Solve," Allen Reed said, tapping Edison's beer bottle with his own, "for X."

Wrapped in a towel like a little chieftan, Toby waddled up and leaned between his father's legs for a moment, his wet hair sweet on Edison's face. Then he called his sister's name suddenly and ran back in to play.

"Right." Edison did not know what to say. He picked up Toby's wet towel in both hands and looked at the men.

Later, as the party was breaking up and the friends clustered at the gate, Dan Hanover said, "It's a relief to have you joining the real world," and Allen Reed clamped his arm around Edison and said, "It's been a good run. You're a hell of a guy."

Melissa Reed took his upper arm against her new bosom and said, "Don't listen to him, Edison. He says that because you remind him of what he was like ten years ago." She squeezed Edison's arm and kissed him on the lips, but his face had fallen.

That night after everyone had left, Edison was agitated and distracted while they cleaned up. He shadowed Leslie around the deck and through the house and at some point he dumped a load of towels in the laundry room and continued on into his study. After Leslie had cleared the patio, blown out all the candle-lanterns, and squared the kitchen away, she found Edison at his desk. She stood in the doorway for a minute, but he was rapt on his calculations.

He was there through the night, working, as he was in the morning and all the long afternoon. He accepted a tuna sandwich about midday. She found him asleep at five P.M., his face on the large sheet of paper surrounded by his animated figurings and the nubs of six pencils.

She helped him into bed, where he woke at midnight with a tiny start that opened Leslie's eyes. "Greetings," she said.

His voice was rocky and uneven. "I went back in. I walked all the way over the low hills, and I climbed up and back over and into the woods—I found the same woods—and I gathered most of the little people. They're like children, I mean, sometimes they follow, and so now I think I'm headed the right way." He sighed heavily and she could hear the fatigue in his chest.

"Get some sleep."

He was whispering. "I don't have them all, and I see now that's part of it; I'm not sure you ever get them all. There are mountains beyond these I didn't even know about."

Leslie lay still. He knew she was awake.

"But that's another time. Now I can keep these guys together and come down. Do you see? I can wrap this up." She was silent, so he added, "There weren't any bears."

"Stop," she said quietly. "You don't want that game."

"It took all night, but I was able to find them because I knew you were waiting." Leslie could hear the ghost of the old exhilaration in his voice.

"Edison," she said, taking his hand. "I'm not there. You need to understand that I'm not at the silver bus anymore. I waited. I saw you give up. Why would I wait?"

"Where'd you go?" There were seconds between all the sentences. "Where are you?"

She spoke slowly. "I don't know. I'm . . . It's way north. I'm in town, living in a small town above the hardware store in an apartment."

He rose to an elbow and she could feel him above her as he spoke. "What's it like there? How far is it?"

"I just got here. No one knows me. It's getting colder. I wear a coat when I walk to the library in the afternoons. I've got to get the kids in school."

Edison lay back down and she heard the breath go out of him. "In town," he said. "Are the leaves turning?"

"Listen." Now she rolled and covered him, a knee over, her arm across his chest. "My landlord asked about you."

"Who? He asked about me?"

"Where my husband was." Leslie put her hand on his shoulder and pulled herself up to kiss him. Held it. "How long I'd be in town."

"And you told him I was lost? He likes you."

"He's a nice man." Leslie shifted up again and now spoke

looking down into his eyes. "He said no one could survive in those hills. Winter comes early. He admired you, your effort." She kissed him. "But you weren't the first person lost to the snow."

"He's been to your place?" Edison's arms were up around her now, and she moved in concert with him.

"He's the landlord." She kissed him deeply, and her hands were moving. "He likes my coffee."

"I always liked your coffee." Edison shifted and pulled her nightshirt over her head, her sudden skin quickening the dark.

"Edison," Leslie whispered. "You're not a hell of a guy; you're not like any of them. Don't join the team." She had been still while she spoke, and now she ran her hand up, finally stopping with her first finger on his nose. "Don't solve for X. Just get all your little people to the bus and drive to town." She pressed her forehead against his. "I left the keys."

"I know where they are," he said. His hand was at her face now, too, and then along her hip, the signal, and he turned them, rolled so that he looked down into her familiar eyes.

"Were you scared?" she said. "What was it like when it started to snow and you were still lost?"

"Everything went white. I wanted to see you again." Every word was sounded against her skin, her hair. "It didn't seem particularly cold, but the snowflakes, when they started, there were trillions."

AT THE JIM BRIDGER

HE PARKED HIS TRUCK IN the gravel in front of the Jim Bridger Lodge, and when he stepped out into the chilly dark, the dog in the back of the rig next to his was a dog who knew him. A lot of the roughnecks had dogs; you saw them standing in the bed of the four-wheel-drive Fords. It was kind of an outfit: the mud-spattered vehicle, the gear in back, a dog. This was a brown and white Australian shepherd who stood and tagged Donner on the arm with his nose, and when the man turned, the dog eyed him and nodded, or so it seemed. What the dog had done is step up on the wheel well and put his head out to be stroked.

"Scout," Donner said, and with a hand on the dog, he scanned the truck. Donner was four hundred miles from home. He knew the truck, too.

Donner had just come out of the mountains after a week fishing with a woman who was not his wife, and that woman now came around the front of Donner's vehicle. He stopped her. She smiled and came into his arms thinking this was another of his little moments. He'd been talking about a cocktail and a steak at the Jim Bridger for days, building it up, playing the expert the way he did with everything. She was on his turf, and he tried to make each moment a ritual with all of his talking. He had more words than anyone she knew. Around the campfires at night, which he built with too much care, he'd make soup and fry fish and offer her a little of the special brandy in a special glass, measured exactly, and he would talk about what night means and what this food before them would allow them to do and how odd it would be to sit in a chair in the Jim Bridger the night of their wacky end-of-season New Year's Eve party and order the big T-bone steak and eat it with a baked potato, which he would also describe in detail.

It was September and they'd gone in twelve miles, back-packing from the trailhead at Valentine Lake. A quarter mile from his truck, he'd stopped and put a burlap bag of Pacifico bottles in the stream that fed Valentine. "We'll be glad to see those on Friday," he told her. "That is my favorite bag in the world; I've pulled it out of twenty creeks, and every time it was full of cold beer."

And that is what they had done today in the late afternoon, their legs sore. They'd walked through the sunny pines for two hours, no speaking, and then he'd stopped and when she caught him, he knelt and pulled the dripping bag and its treasure into the sunlight. They sat on the bank and he opened the bottles with his knife. The cold brown bottles were slippery in their hands, the labels washed off, and they were like two people having their first beer on earth. She put her hand on the wet burlap. It was all as good as he'd said it would be.

They were both changed from the trip in ways they didn't understand. He was fighting a kind of terror that had grown, and now as he ran his hand under Scout's collar and scratched the animal, the feeling rose and tightened his throat.

"I know somebody in here," he said to her.

"I know you do." she said. "Happy New Year." She kissed him. She had given herself over to him sometime at midweek and was not even fighting the love that had taken her.

"No," he said, "really. I know this guy." He indicated the big truck. "I know this dog, Scout."

"Scout?" She'd heard about this dog.

"Right," he said. "The dog from the story."

She put both arms around him and asked, "Does this mean we don't get our steak?"

With the euphoric bravado that had infected the whole adventure, he put his cold hand under her sweatshirt and pulled her up and kissed her in front of the dog. Then he took her hand and led her into the big log tavern he'd been talking about for five days. The two windows in front were lined with tiny celebration lights and foil letters read *Happy New Year!* The season always ended this weekend at the Jim Bridger: they pulled the dock up onto the shore of Long Pond behind the place and packed all the patio tables and chairs in a barn off to one side, and celebrated New Year's Eve a hundred and twenty days early.

Inside there were two little rooms, the small barroom with eight stools and, past a kind of narrow passage, the dining room, which held a scattering of tables, each with a red checked tablecloth, just as he had told her. A dozen trophy heads protruded from the walls, twelve- and fourteen-point deer and over the fireplace a bull elk that would have gone a thousand pounds. There was no one in the bar, though there were oil-field and hunting jackets on every stool, and bottles and glasses standing all along the wooden surface, as if everyone had left suddenly mid-drink. Brenda Lee sang from the jukebox, "Fool Number One." It was full of scratch friction as if coming across the decades to find the room. The dining hall, too, was empty, though there were steak dinners on two of the tables and coats on some of the chairs. Donner sat the woman at a table, and then he saw something through the big back windows. They were flocked with white and gold spray and razored with a loopy script that read *Happy New Year!* Through the words Donner could see a group of people out on the wooden deck looking into Long Pond. "They're all out back," he said. "Some deal out back."

Donner had told the woman the second day of the trip that he had memorized her, her back, the backs of her knees, the scar on her shoulder, her navel, her nipples, how her hair grew, the way she looked immediately after stepping out of her clothes, the way she looked an hour later. But as they opened the plastic menus in the dark little room and he looked across at her beneficent smile, he didn't even know who she was. This had all been accomplished on a rushing wave of what, adrenaline? Lust? Ego? Now that had collapsed and Donner felt ruined and hollow. He felt as if he'd used every gesture, every smile, and he knew that everything he did now was something borrowed.

"There it is," she said, pointing at the menu. She was euphoric. She'd been euphoric for days. "T-bone steak with a baked potato."

"There it is," he said.

The door opened and the conversation noise roared in like a draft and then people followed it in, one and two at a time. Donner saw Rusty right away holding the door for a couple of his buddies, and Donner turned his back and faced the woman until he was sure they had passed through the room and back to the bar.

The waitress was the owner's wife, Kay. Donner knew her name, but she didn't know his. He was here once a year at most. She appeared in a big flannel shirt patterned red and black and a shiny tiara clipped on her head that in rhinestones read *Happy New Year!* and she kept the pencil, as he had described to the woman, behind her ear until she'd heard both their orders and then she wrote it down.

"What was that?" Donner asked her about the people coming in.

"Big Jess our bull moose made an appearance across the pond," Kay told him. "He's still over there pulling tall grass off the bottom and eating like there's no tomorrow."

"A moose?" the woman said. "We saw a moose."

"We did," Donner said.

Early the second day, still hiking toward their lake, they had passed through a willow break, and in one of the beaver dams a cow moose was feeding. She was standing to her shoulders in the water, and her huge head would descend and disappear and then emerge in a tremendous splash and her mouth would be full of dark green reeds and she would chew and drip. It thrilled the woman, and she covered her face with her hands. She looked at Donner with a radical amazement, as if her understanding of the world had been reset, and she pulled him over a hillock and dropped her pack. They came together in a way that shocked him, none of it something he could easily describe, not voracious and not tender, but seriously perhaps, and it sobered him and offered the first caution as to the nature of what he was actually doing.

The waitress brought back a bread basket and two plastic flutes of champagne. There was a little stone fireplace and Donner stoked the struggling fire with two fresh sections of split log. When he sat back down, she said, "So this is New Year's."

"It is."

She scanned the room. "And they'll close the shutters and all be gone tomorrow."

"Right, until May first. But even that is early. The season here doesn't start until June."

Her eyes were on him, and she lifted her glass and held it until he touched it with his. She was waiting for him to say something, make a toast.

"Moose," he said. "God save the moose."

Now he saw her first confusion, and he worried she could read his face. He felt drained, but he smiled.

"Is that really Scout?" she said. "Isn't that amazing?"

"Yes it is, my dear," he said.

"So, is your friend in here?"

"Yes," he said. "He's sitting at the bar."

"Rusty?"

"That's his name," he said. "You remembered."

He didn't want to talk about this, but he would if she wanted, because he realized that he didn't want to talk about anything at all. From the moment the dog had touched him, everything was all gone. Donner was happy for the fire; if the grate had been dark, he feared he would have wept.

One year ago in September on Donner's annual fishing trip, he'd gotten trapped by a surprise snowstorm in the Cascades, and he'd made a bad decision. It was now his favorite story, though he'd only told it twice, and when he told it, he told it carefully and honestly, owning all of his errors in the event. When he told it, something in him knitted up taut and he felt centered and ready. He had told the woman who was not his wife the story over dinner at an Italian restaurant seven months ago, and it was the story that had kindled all of the rest.

The big mistake Donner made while fishing the year before, larger than going into the mountains late in the year and getting caught by the four-day storm, was breaking camp late in the afternoon. He should have stayed put, as he had for three days while the snowfall continued without pause, steady and serious as if trying to put the year out once and for all.

He had arrived in a thick dusk and set up camp—the tent, the little cook station and grill, the log bench, the clothesline. He always had a clothesline, and on the clothesline he always hung a thin cotton dish towel bordered by a blue and green stripe. His mother had given it to him years before. He woke the first day in the strange quiet and even light and his tent half in on him. The snow was eight inches deep, and Donner had to dress carefully and search through the site for his gear. He broke dead limbs and made a small fire; he was a scrupulous fire maker, and he laid in wood for two days. He made a cup of coffee using the little press his wife had given him, and he brushed a space on the log and sat down and let the snow gather on his shoulders.

He had the wrong shoes for such weather, but by being prudent and drying them each time he returned to the fire, he was still able to fish in Native Lake. He was mindful of the wet rocks and stood with his legs angled on the last two and cast a series of flies into the blizzard. It was mesmerizing watching the snow in its vast echelons disappear into the dark water, and he had the rich, high feeling that comes from being alone in real places. He caught no fish on his flies.

He did, however, take several cutthroat trout on his smallest Mepps spinners, something they could see. These fish he fried slowly in his old pan with olive oil and a little tarragon, and he ate them with his fingers right out of the pan as snow still fell. At night he banked the fire with larger logs, and in the morning snow would cover them all but one small space where smoke would still be working its way into the cold new day.

He fished every year of his life, camping alone or with a partner, because, he said, it pinned everything else in his life in place. He came home tight with the regimen of sleeping on the ground and eating fish, and with a new effulgent appreciation for his house, the roof, the way the doors worked, chairs.

The year of the mistake he'd gone into the mountains under special pressure. Andrew, his fourteen-year-old son, had run away that spring and then come back, and then run off again. It had been a poisonous season of recrimination and fear. He had been a drummer in the school marching band, and then he was just gone and they did not know where.

In twelve years this had been the first snow, and though he wasn't fully unprepared, it vexed him. He wished he had his gaiters. He ate cutthroat trout for three days, drank coffee, and on the fourth day, he made his mistake. In the low, even snow light, which was the same at nine A.M. as it was in midafternoon, he decided that he could no longer wait out the snow. Even if it stopped, it would be a week melting in the best of Indian summers. He would hike down halfway to the highway, seven miles, camp there overnight, and then continue down another seven to the highway where the bus had let him off.

He waited and waited, and then for some reason he broke camp late in the fourth day. He should have waited for morning, but he could not. When he pulled the tent and packed it, the little rectangle under it was green as summer, the grass and wildflowers pressed and vivid there like a window onto another world.

He knew he'd made the mistake immediately because of the difficulty locating and keeping the trail. There were yellow blazes hacked into trees at the proper intervals, but the pack trail was impossible to see in the two-foot snow. The rocks tripped him, and he learned in the first mile to simply fall when he stepped on the side of the angled rocks rather than struggle for balance. Game trails confused him and many times he'd follow an elk path and then fifty yards later come face-to-face with a tree the animal would have walked under; he'd have to backtrack in the growing gloom to locate the proper path. He was wet, but moving and warm. When dark took the sky, the snow persisted. He used his flashlight to find the marked trees.

As he had told the story to the woman in the Italian restaurant last February, it lived in him, each word, and he evoked the dark and the night and the snow. He told the next part with complete precision, how he'd followed the trail, breathing into the new night, and suddenly plunged into the huge open meadow. He had forgotten about it. The expanse glowed at him, offering no marker; the trail was lost. He walked into the snow field for some reason. Was he looking for a clue? He moved slowly now, regretting having left the trees, tramping through the powdered snow. A moment later he came to a rivulet he seemed to remember, the water amber and clear, and he walked right into it and watched the water flow over his boots. He was now somebody else, somebody he was curious about. It was a beautiful night, the snow now tiny dots still wandering, floating all around the man. Habit, he supposed, not a decision, but habit made him walk into the snow toward the distant trees. He was trying to take care. He looked at his watch, which he was trained to do when confused or lost, but a moment later he couldn't remember what it had said. He looked again, wiping the crystal with his gloved first finger. He swore at the instrument and walked on, each step a kick into the deep drifts, listening to himself cursing. He fell frequently on the uneven ground, and the falling filled his collar with snow and then his ear. Sometimes he'd stay down; he wasn't cold anymore.

He didn't remember getting up, but he was up and in the woods, his pack off, breaking dead limbs from trees, and he was on his knees with his fire kit, starting a fire with a little snarl of twigs, a fire that he nursed into the biggest fire he'd had all week.

As the fire grew in his story, the woman's expression, which was already serious in the restaurant candlelight, grew grave, her eyes on his face, glistening.

His fire worked its way down through the snow to the green forest floor and grew out in a dry circle. He pulled a downed limb over and hung his wet clothing on it piece by piece until he was standing on his towel before the vigorous fire naked, the dots of snow burning on his shoulders. He made some soup and set up his tent while his clothes dried. Hunkered down in the circle of warmth he had created, sipping the steaming tomato soup, he felt as alive as he ever had.

It was about one minute later a dog burst into the bright ring, throwing a splash of snow before putting his iced muzzle onto his paws on the only patch of green grass in this whole world. The dog eyed the naked man. There had been no noise in the arrival, and Donner was sure at first that a coyote had made a mistake, but he stood his ground. When he saw what it was, he said, "Hello, boy," and his voice sounded strange. Donner found the tags and collar frozen, and by the time he'd separated them and read *Scout*, and a Wyoming phone number, he heard a deep voice call from the dark, "Hello, the camp!" When Rusty Patrick stamped into the light, he looked at Donner and pulled his snow-crusted glove off to shake hands. "Well, here's Adam. Is Eve in the tent?"

Donner pulled on his cotton pajama bottoms, which he always took camping. This last week when he erected their camp clothesline and hung up the dish towel, he had also pinned the pajamas to the line and the woman had taken the fabric in her hand and Donner could see her remembering the story.

But in the Italian restaurant last February, when she first heard about the snow camp, the ring of snow, the way it melted, she said, "I want that. I want to have that."

The steaks in the Jim Bridger were big, an end over each side of the huge paper plates, and the baked potatoes were monstrous. The only real silverware was the three-tined fork Kay brought them and pocketknives. It was a trademark of the Bridger to give pocketknives for steaks. They were thick black Forest Master knives with three blades, but the nameplate on each read *Bridger Club*. The woman loved this, and though she didn't look comfortable with the pocketknife, she went at the food with an energy and delectation that Donner envied.

All night long they'd shared the fun of the place, diners getting up and throwing their plates into the fireplace and toasting, "Happy New Year!"

"They're not doing any dishes the last night of the year," Donner had told her.

When she talked now, her mouth was full, chewing, smiling, and Donner knew he had done it double. She was a woman who didn't talk with her mouth full, ever. She was in love and it was his doing. When Kay passed with the bottle, the woman held out her glass for more champagne, and Donner could see her beam. She was beaming.

A three-piece band was setting up in the corner, wiring the keyboard, as Donner and the woman finished their dinner.

"Are you going to speak to him?" she asked Donner. "Do I get to meet Rusty Patrick?"

The second thing Rusty Patrick had said to Donner a year ago in the snow camp was, "I've had a pretty weird month all around." He worked a black revolver from his jacket pocket and showed it to Donner. There were frost starts in the bluing. Rusty hefted the gun and then lobbed it out over the fire into the snow. "I was dead for a while, but I guess I'm back. Do you know how fucking strange it was to see your fire? I came out of the trees and there's this fire. Come on. Whose idea is that?"

After he'd had a cup of soup, he added, "But we're still in plenty of trouble here." His Levi's were frozen in stiff sheets and his boot laces were welded with ice. He kicked and beat at his clothing to peel it off, hanging it to dry. He'd been out to climb Mount Warren and had hit it way too light. Both of his little toes were patched white with crystal frostbite, but he stood by the fire in his damp long underwear and toasted the falling snow with his coffee cup. "People in Sun Valley pay a thousand dollars a day for shit like this."

Donner did not mention the gun when he told the story, and he did not tell the woman or anyone else what happened the night he met Rusty Patrick in the snow camp. As the snow continued, they had another cup of coffee with a lick of whiskey in it, and they decided to walk out in the morning. With two of them, they reasoned, they could take turns breaking trail. They were above eleven thousand feet, and they were still ten miles from the road. Donner had set his tent on the snow, not bothering to kick a clearing for it, and none of the tree wells were large enough for the little two-man spring tent.

He felt odd, wired and wasted, and he understood somewhere deeper than he could reach that when he had seen the dog, he had let go of all the prudence he'd garnered all day. He was tired. Rusty Patrick wanted to talk and did talk for the hour they lay in the tent. Donner felt the snow hardening under them as they settled, and he worried faintly about the cold, but he just lay back and listened.

Rusty Patrick had a resonant voice, so even his speaking voice scraped a hard bass note once or twice in every sentence. He was a roughneck driving truck since the oil work had dried up. Now he hauled road gravel all over Wyoming. "They're still blading roads," he said. "That's why there isn't an unbroken windshield in this whole state." At thirty-three, he had never been married, never had a real girl until this last summer when he fell in love with the new dispatcher, a woman named Darlene Youngman, who had come west from Pennsylvania. It was the story of this girl that he told Donner.

Rusty Patrick talked in the icy tent, stopping every once in a while to post a question. Donner was awake but not enough to answer, and after a pause, Rusty Patrick would continue. His heart was broken, he said. He used to think that was all bullshit, a broken heart, before this deal. He fell in love with Darlene Youngman and she fell in love with him, and their dating closed in on them until they were spending weekends together at his place in Rawlins or hers in Rock Springs. "I mean, I see now that love is a kind of craziness, right? I was lit up like a refinery at night, blazing, nothing like it. It made everything make sense. My stupid life, the unending wind, the great state of Wyoming. You ever been in love?" Rusty cleaned himself up, his bachelor apartment, his clothing, his truck, and he trimmed his mustache and got out the old Western Wyoming College bulletins that had been in a drawer for six years. He was planning on a career in the Forest Service.

The dog came to the mouth of the tent and looked Donner in the eye. Donner nodded his head and the dog stepped carefully in onto the sleeping bags, finally curling at their knees.

The resonant cadence of Rusty Patrick's voice changed

then, or so Donner thought from where he drifted listening.
He wanted to drop into sleep, and he could have, but there
was something holding him back, some caution, some change
in the air and the grip of the snowpack beneath him.

"My boss was a good guy—at least he had been good to
me, keeping me on when a lot of men were laid off. His name
was Bob Baxter. He took me aside years ago and told me pri-
vately to get my big-rig license, and I did what he said, and it
saved me. But there was something else. He took an interest
in Darlene." The company owner felt fatherly toward the
young woman, and in all their hours together in the office,
the man talked against Rusty Patrick, warning the woman
about a man of his caliber. It was a steady lesson, an
onslaught, and she didn't tell Rusty Patrick about it right
away. Then one weekend two weeks ago, he'd taken her over
to the Western campus at Rock Springs, just driving around
with a school map so he wouldn't get lost when he came here
next year. He was excited. Their new life was diagrammed
before them. He would move in with her and attend classes;
he had nine thousand dollars in the bank and he could work
part-time in town during the two-year forestry program.
Then they'd go together down to Utah State or Colorado State
and their lives would really begin. He was thinking about
babies and had said as much. He was way in, far gone. That's
the way he had said it, "I was far gone. I mean, I'd brought up
babies. I'd say anything and I meant it all." They were walking across the windy campus when she stopped and told him
quietly that he would never come here. He was surprised by
this and asked her why. This is not something you'll do, she
told him. Her arms were folded and she went directly to his
truck. It was early on Saturday, so many sweet hours ahead of
them, but she sat stone still. When she didn't talk, he didn't
talk, and he drove her home. When she walked to her door, he
simply backed his rig up and drove home. His ears were ring-

ing. He hadn't talked to her since, but he'd gone in to see his boss. "I went to the office on that Saturday," Rusty whispered. "And Baxter was waiting for me."

Donner could feel Rusty's shoulder; he was crying, speaking sometimes through his teeth. "By then I was like a chunk of stone; it hurt so bad. There is nothing like it. It isn't your heart; it's your heart through every day of your goddamned life. I could understand why a woman like Darlene might want to leave a man like me alone, but I was sure that Bob Baxter. Would not. Have said anything. Against me."

Rusty trembled for a while, breathing as if gathering steam for language. "He told me. He had told her. I was no good. For her. He told me hehadbeen talking. To her since. He had found out we were dating."

Rusty's voice was quieter and the words were spaced oddly, some run together and some repeated shakily and some falling at great intervals. The new cadence woke Donner a level. "It took everything. I had. Not to kill the man," Rusty said. "AndIcouldhavekilledhim with my my my fists. My life was over. I bought the gun. Fourhundredbucks. That was. Tuesday. We've been up above here. Since. Then. In this this this this snow."

The last word had been coughed out and immediately Rusty's breathing changed to a shallow chuffing. It was late but the hard chill pressed in with a new edge; it had stopped snowing. Donner opened his eyes and listened, and he knew that after four days it had stopped snowing. The cold came down now with all the force of the hollow sky. He could feel the frigid air sizing his face, and his feet were aching again.

The story had made him sick. He imagined the big boyish figure of Rusty Patrick confronting an older man he thought of as a father and hearing such news. And the surprise of the surcease of falling snow was like terror, a blank, fearful void that came at Donner's heart. He tried to calm himself, but for the first time in the mountains he was afraid. It was very simple: he wanted to be home. The image of his son in his band uniform took the air from Donner's lungs, the brass buttons on his red wool tunic, his high, proud face under the black beret, his seriousness with the snare drum. He wouldn't even accept any help loading the drums in the car, and when they arrived at school, he went wordlessly into the crowd. And then he disappeared. One night after practice, Donner waited with his wife, and after one A.M., they called the police.

Donner was bumped from sleep by Rusty Patrick shaking beside him. At first Donner thought the other man was sobbing, because he had heard it in his voice earlier, but it persisted, a rippling shudder that wasn't crying. "Hey," Donner had said, but even on an elbow shaking the man, Donner couldn't wake Rusty Patrick. The dog held tight at the bottom of the sleeping bags, his eyes open. The cold was at Donner, blades of it against his exposed neck as he moved up and checked the other man. He ran a hand over Rusty's face and it came away wet, and then cold or no, Donner sat up on his heels and shined the light on his tent mate. The face was gray and smeared with blood from a nosebleed. A delicate fringe of ice rimmed the hair and Rusty Patrick was shivering in cramping spasms. His chest was wet. Donner was saying, "Come on, come on," as he unzipped their sleeping bags. The other man was damp, cold to the touch, dropping into hypothermia. Both of Donner's hands were bloody and he was getting the blood everywhere as he cut away Rusty's underwear using his sheath knife. Both of the sleeping bags were superior grade, though the zippers wouldn't mesh. Donner was talking the whole time now, saying simply, "Oh now, come on now," and he slipped in with Rusty and wrapped the shell of his own bag over them as tightly as he could. It was what you did. There was no way to take the half hour to

rekindle the fire and go that way. Patrick had gone to bed still
wet and it had worked into him. Now Donner could feel the
cold muscularity of the other man and he held him and
moved slowly against him, his hands up and down, the tops of
his feet up and down, his face against the side of Rusty
Patrick's head. He'd need to bring him up five degrees.

Even dozing, he developed a rhythm, covering the naked
body of Rusty Patrick in this embrace, this massage. It wore
him down and he felt useless. He woke and renewed his
movements. Donner rolled on top of Rusty and in slow
degrees as his strength left him, he let his weight descend.
The dog moved up to them, and Donner could feel the dog's
breath against the side of his face. Rusty's shivering had subsided somewhat, but Donner could still feel the blood warm
against his neck.

"Come on, now," he said, whispering, and when that litany
lulled him to sleep, he started talking quietly to his son. "You
can come home now," he started. "It's not a problem to cross
through Indiana and then Nebraska . . ." and Donner listed
the states one at a time in a prayer to his son. He spoke slowly,
trying to lay out the fair terms of their rapprochement, so he
might again be some part of his life, and in his recitation, he
uttered their history, telling at length episodes they'd shared,
especially the time they went onto the roof to retrieve the
basketball. He'd gone up the ladder and Andrew had followed
him onto the flat white surface the shape of Utah. It was lit-
tered with odd broken toys and an old volleyball as well as the
ball he'd just heaved from the driveway. Each element of this
scattered inventory brought a wave of revelation and nostal-
gia. The blue plastic elephant with three legs was five or six
years old, sun-polished on one side, and Donner and Andrew
sat on the short rear wall of the roof, looking down at the
neighbors' dog, who was swimming in the pool, and they
talked about all the toys the elephant had been kindred to,

and he asked Donner in real wonder how such a lost thing could get onto the roof. In the late-day shade, they laughed and speculated like two friends for an hour until his wife called them from below.

Donner hugged the freezing man. He trapped Rusty's hands in the warmth between their legs. Their center was warm and Donner moved against it until he felt himself stirred, a reflex he gave in to. Rusty Patrick's breathing had steadied into a rhythmic easy stride cut from time to time with a short shudder. Donner was calling his name now, "Rusty, hey, Rusty." The man beneath him groaned in what might have been acknowledgment and moved, his eyes still shut, and then Donner knew that Rusty had taken him into his hands and they were together that way in the mountain tent.

In the morning Donner saw what he hadn't seen for five days: shadows on the tent, the shocking sunprint of tree limbs on the gray canvas. It warmed to twenty five and then thirty degrees. They took a long time with their morning, boiling water for coffee and oatmeal and then another pan for washing. There was dried blood in their hair and on their faces and necks. The world was a blinding white, the sky blue in tiers to the horizon. They didn't speak, both men packing up carefully and wearing sunglasses against the crushing light. The muted concussions of snow bundles falling from the thawing limbs sounded all around them, and the dog Scout circled in the snow-packed camp space ready to go.

Donner told the woman the rest of the story: the warming, brilliant day in mid-September, and walking out of the mountains with Rusty Patrick and his dog. The dog disappeared right away and then five minutes later came along working two cattle before him like an expert in snow herding. The men stopped to watch this display. Donner took off his jacket and tucked it into his pack. They would walk ten miles downhill on a snow-packed path behind an ever-increasing line of cows which the dog urged and instructed, a kind of rare pleasure that comes once in a lifetime.

In that larger well-lit world with a clear promise of tomorrow and home and hope, Donner thought it might be possible to speak to Rusty Patrick about what had happened, but at each juncture, as they stopped for water or granola bars or just to look the hundred miles east across the snow-patched plains, neither man spoke up except to say, "Some dog," or the like. When they shook hands that evening at the bus station in a town that Donner would never visit again, he thought, I'll never know any of this again, any of it, and I'll never see Rusty Patrick again.

Now in the Jim Bridger, Donner and the woman who was not his wife had thrown their paper plates and steak bones into the fireplace and moved their table to the periphery of the dining room, stacking it upside down on those already there. It was after eleven and people, many wearing gold and silver paper party hats, danced. It was fun for the woman and she held on to Donner's arm happily, pretending every so often to have something to whisper to him and kissing his neck instead. This was all better than he'd described it.

At one point she'd bought an embroidered Jim Bridger cap from the little glass case, a turquoise cap with a moose underneath the name, and she announced it was for Andrew, a present.

"I'm not sure that's a good idea," he said.

"He likes me; this is a good cap for him," the woman had said. He didn't like her using Andrew's name. His wife's name had come up from time to time in the last days, but it was just a fact, one he was steeled against. When she said his son's name, it just confused him.

One of the band members had a full beard and every third song he'd hoist his accordion and announce, "The New Year's Polka," to which they'd already danced twice. Their waitress, Kay, danced every dance now in the warm wooden-floored room, each with a different young man. The employees were all going home and back to college, and she was dancing with them one by one. Donner heard, through all the talking and the music and the dinner noise, the regular bass beat of Rusty Patrick's deep voice as he spoke to his mates in the other room. After a week of knowing what he was doing or pretending to know, Donner was dislocated and floating, his brave face paper thin.

At a few minutes before the hour, all the men from the bar were herded into the dining room by Kay's husband, the bartender, and Kay herself went around and filled everybody's glass with the champagne they'd been pouring all night. "Kay," her husband said, emerging through the group of men, "evidently the clock in the bar has been five minutes fast for the entire year! Thank God we've made it for the toast."

He was hooted down, and in the ringing laughter, Donner saw Rusty Patrick turn and look into his face. Rusty's expression opened in strange surprise and he came immediately over to where Donner and the woman stood by the stone fireplace.

"No way," he said, shaking Donner's hand. Then he said it again and clapped Donner in an embrace. He opened his mouth again to say something, which would have been, *What are you doing here?* or *Is it really you?* but with his mouth open, he just hugged Donner hard again.

They were spilling champagne, and Donner could sense the woman at his arm also against him, but he could not speak. The room seemed to be glowing. Donner could only put his arm around Rusty and hug him again, feeling the whiskers against the bones in his face. When they stood back, Rusty asked the woman, "So, you must be his wife?"

She took his arm in their close circle and said no, she was his friend.

"I'm Rusty," he said.

"I know," she said. "I've heard about you." Now she had her hands on both of his forearms. "I've heard the wonderful story."

"One minute!" the bartender called. "Make amends or wait a year! Who needs champagne! Where's my sweetheart!" His wife, Kay, appeared at his back and they kissed. The room was full, everyone shoulder to shoulder.

Rusty Patrick opened his face to Donner in a profound look, plaintive and deep. A basket full of noisemakers suddenly appeared between them, and the men took one each and started blowing the honking whistles until the accordion sounded the countdown: ten . . . nine . . . eight. The men's look held. Donner felt a smooth hand on his face and the woman pulled him down, and she kissed him tenderly, keeping her hand there as the minute and the hour and the year lapsed for the people in the Jim Bridger. A shotgun sounded from out on the highway, and paper dots fell into everyone's hair.

Immediately the band fired up and the room sorted itself out, alcoves of people widening until the dancers had some space. It was another version of "The New Year's Polka."

Rusty's buddies all slipped back into the bar, but Rusty Patrick came to Donner, speaking in his ear. "How's your son?" the man said, his voice full of real concern. "Did he make it home? Did you talk to him?"

Donner could only nod at Rusty then and drop his eyes and step back. The young woman who was not his wife had snugged the turquoise cap onto her head and threaded her hair out the back in a ponytail. "Let's dance!" she called in the thrumming noise. "I haven't danced all year!"

Donner was watching what his body did, and what it did now was push Rusty and the woman together and smile at them. "Go to it!" he said. "This runs a thousand dollars a day in Sun Valley. I'm going to get some air."

The night was ripped, filled, upended with stars sizzling in the deep chill. Donner felt his scalp tighten against the gathering cold, and he blew great plumes into the air. He retrieved his binoculars from his car kit, and when he shut the door, the dog stood in Rusty's truck to be stroked.

"Come on, Scout," Donner said, patting his leg. "Let's go see the moose."

Scout stood two feet on the tailgate and Donner lifted the animal to the ground rather than have him jump. They walked around the side of the old Jim Bridger to the wooden deck over Long Pond. There were two people finishing an argument as he arrived and the woman said to the man, "That's four strikes, Artie, and you damn well know it." They went in, releasing a quick rush of noise.

The binoculars had belonged to Donner's father and they were the best set he'd ever seen. He sighted Big Jess standing well into the trees on the far side. Donner breathed out and held so he could focus. The moose wasn't moving, and Donner couldn't tell if he was looking across at the party.

Certain decisions are made in daylight and certain decisions are made in darkness. Winter has its own decisions and summer has its own decisions, as do spring and fall. Donner drew a chestful of the sharp air. He'd made a decision last February with the woman whom he could now see dancing inside the painted window. It was made in the frigid early twilight under low clouds while the car headlamps passing on the highway seemed useless little fires that wouldn't last the night, and that decision to use his story as he had, to show it to her, burn it like a match, had led to this new darkness and the longer night.

THE CLICKER AT TIPS

BY THE TIME I PULLED open the big wooden door of Tips, Eve had finished off a third of the English beer menu. She was sitting dead center in the middle of the big empty bar-room like a lost child. On the other side of the bar station two guys played pool at one of the twelve tables. The floor in Tips was varnished cement; it was not a very comfortable place, but they filled it every night with all the young brokers who were still in mourning for college.

"Did you notice how there's no work anymore?" she said when I sat down. "This place used to be a factory."

"I work," I said

"No you don't. You fly around and talk for money."

"Eve," I said. "You don't think air travel is work?"

"You get introduced, walk to the podium, always a nicer piece of furniture than I have in my whole house, and then you pause a beat because you're sure that every eye is on you, then you pause again and then you give your lecture. After-ward they hand you a big check. They pay you for those pauses."

There was an edge in it; I could hear it, but Eve always had an edge. I had wanted to see her; it had been two months, silence since our last meeting, dinner downtown. I was sur-prised that her mention of her house, the rooms of which I knew well, had quickened everything.

The waitress came over, a tall young woman with long braids. "Did one of you guys want the clicker?"

"*Moi,*" Eve said, presenting her palm. The girl placed the television remote control in it. The five televisions around the room were all set on the pregame show. I asked the waitress for a pint of Bass and a platter of the wings.

"Are we on television?" I asked Eve.

"We are. We're on the six-fifteen."

"Who are you scolding today?"

"That same sleazeball with the jewelry."

"What did he say?"

"He was able to push me down and stride nobly to his Lexus. That's why I want to see it." Eve was ombudsman for Channel 14, sniffing out consumer complaints. Last week she'd put a bottled water company out of business, and this week it was this guy Gene Somebody and his fake Navajo jewelry.

"Are you all right?"

"I'm fine. I sat on my ass in Scottsdale and did the report and realized I hadn't been pushed to the ground since you took that privilege two years ago."

"Eve," I said.

"Let's have another pint." She was speaking over my head to the waitress, who came round and set my beer smoothly on the table. "But something from the Continent now. Something from some country that doesn't even exist anymore."

"Pardon?" the waitress said.

"Eve wants the Yugoslavian lager," I told her. I looked at my full glass. "Make it two."

"Yes, the little hero comes to the door, sees the mike, and bolts. Some sixty-year-old in tight jeans pushes me down. I just want to see it. Is this a soulless place or is it me?" She drank and looked at me. "God, what a word and me to use it."

"It will have soul in a thousand years."

"Should we wait? Pardon: Should I wait?" She pointed the remote at the television near us and it flipped forward to fourteen, where our pal Jeff Nederhaller was anchoring the news with Monica Young. Jeff and I had been part of a pretty tight circle a few years before; we had all worked at the newspaper.

I said, "Jeff looks good. Everyone should get divorced."

"He's nuts. He is an outright idiot. Marriage keeps people fat and sane."

"Very fine. So I'm sane."

Eve drilled me with a look. "Oh, are you married?"

"Eve," I said. "Let's have a nice time. Let's have a few beers and a nice time."

Around us the place was filling with the *Monday Night Football* crowd, clusters of six and eight people pushing tables together, hanging their coats on the backs of the heavy wooden school chairs, ordering pitchers of imported beer. The group beside us watching the corner TV all wore blue blazers and pin-striped shirts, a kind of uniform, young guys with great hair, talking loudly and making bets on the Bears. Some of them were from Chicago. There were days when everyone in Phoenix seemed to be from Chicago.

"Laborers," Eve said. "Stevedores."

"Middle management from Motorola," I said.

"Longshoremen, teamsters." She looked at me and said, "Oh, don't be so smug. Take your jacket off, let's see your stripes."

I did, hanging my tweed coat on the chair. She scanned my black polo shirt and said, "You dress like an actor."

I considered commenting on her sleek silk dress, dark green, the black sash around her waist, how she looked good, dressed not to kill but certainly to harm, and in the half second I had that thought it settled on me just how good she looked, not the dress but the choice of it. She was beautiful, smart; she looked in every way superior. She was impeccable, always. No wonder the scared little guy pushed her down.

"You're dressed like a guy whose latest movie we should have clips of, someone who flew in from the coast. The whole world's a talk show."

"That it is."

"So, Matt, what's your latest project?" She wanted me to start being clever, to fence, to fight.

"You called, I came along."

"Such power." She drank her beer and narrowed her eyes. "Out of affection or fear?" The room was picking up, voices through the muffled waves of clicking pool balls.

"Eve, you're wearing me out." I toasted her. "I was thirsty."

After a car commercial, there she was on the screen in that green dress, holding the microphone in front of her face. She looked smart and serious, and when she pointed behind her to the storefront, Anazazi Gems, in the sunny little strip mall, and turned, the camera followed her. The man in jeans had just emerged and was locking the glass door when Eve stepped back in frame, poised if not smug, and said, "Mr. Fuller, Eve Moran from *Channel 14 News*. We've had your genuine Indian jewelry analyzed by two independent experts and they're telling us that it's imported. Could you tell—" This is when Fuller bolted and we saw the sky for a moment as the camera was jarred, and then there was a tilted shot of Mr. Fuller boarding his silver Lexus and then an unsteady pan back to Eve sitting in the gravel of the little parking island. She didn't miss a beat. She didn't even try to get up, but turned her legs to one side as if she were sitting on the deck of a yacht and went on, "We tried to contact Mr. Fuller's workshop in Payson, but the phone was disconnected some time ago and the address we received is that of the Sunshine Laundry and Dry Cleaners, which has been at their location for more than twenty years." Sitting like that, holding the mike up, her knees to one side, Eve looked beautiful. "In Scottsdale, this is Eve Moran, Ombudsman, *Channel 14 News.*"

The screen went back to the console two-shot of Jeff Nederhaller and Monica Young and they said something, a joke about the news being a rough business, and thanked Eve for that report.

"Fabulous," I said, meaning it. "And you're okay?"

"I took Chuck for margaritas at a little place two doors down, a dive. He got a black eye from that bump on the camera."

"Chuck's a good guy," I said. "This is two lawsuits and a written apology."

"Please. It's a black eye, a sore ass, and the afternoon off." She smiled. "Though I do think that was a stunning report. Did you see that gravel?"

"You're something else."

"Again, please. Save that for someone you're willing to seduce." She looked at me over her glass. "Although I'm glad to hear you still love me. How's Debbie?"

"How's Debbie?" I said the name and felt it ring the way your wife's name rings in such places at such times. "Debbie is fine," I said. "She's still working with the utility commission. Debbie's fine. She's having a success actually."

"We never thought anything but success for that girl." I could hear the faint echo of those margaritas in Eve's voice; she was a little drunk.

The game had come on all over the bar except for on our television, which was now showing *Hard Copy*. In the corner near us the group of young regulars had circled their chairs around two of the little tables and were making noises about Chicago this, Arizona that, even though it was going to be a one-sided exhibition. There were five or six guys. They leaned back in their chairs and pointed at the screen from time to time, yucking it up. They got to me for all the wrong reasons. I didn't envy them so much as want to correct them, ask them to display some real comaraderie, some real something the way I had with my friends Eve and David and Christopher and Jeff and Deborah, now Debbie, my wife. We had met in magical ways and hung out in the real places like a kind of family over an evening of drinks and appetizers, plate after plate, and we had talked wickedly, tenderly, and we all knew that those hours once or twice a week were our real lives, the center. One thing led to another; there was a sense of things happening. I hated these young guys and their surface lives, a night with the football game. I hated the evening coming on this way, and my life, one good part of it, over.

"You're looking anemic," Eve said. "Sorry you came? I haven't seen you in what? Two months."

"I'm fine," I said, finishing my beer. I signaled the waitress and she stopped. "Let's have some Red Stripe," I told her.

"And a little tequila?" Eve said. "You always like a shot with your Red Stripe."

Her remembering tapped me a little, but I didn't miss a beat. "Right, then," I said. "Shots." The young woman and her braids went off. "What do you hear from Christopher?"

"Christopher has not called me," Eve said. "My sources tell me he's become a naked careerist at the paper, kissing editorial butt long into the night."

Christopher had taken the features job at the paper and had his little photograph above the keystone column twice a week. When he first got on, Eve used to clip the picture and affix it to envelopes like a stamp and drop them by the various offices with a phony cancellation.

"He doesn't need to do that; he's the best writer they've got. If we'd stayed, we might have learned to write."

"A dripping success like the rest." Eve lifted the remote and began leafing through the channels.

"Are they going to show your assault again at ten?" I asked her.

"I'm afraid it's the only news they've got, unless there's been a solution in Bosnia." She stopped at a black-and-white screen: the ocean, a frigate in a gray studio gale. Errol Flynn was in trouble on the high seas. "Jesus," Eve said, "look. A real movie about real work."

"I'm not sure."

"It's a real ship in real jeopardy, storm tossed. Every man on that vessel is thinking about his god."

"That vessel is five feet long, being tossed by a wave machine in a studio pool."

The waitress came and set our drinks on the table; there was now a city of glasses. I touched Eve's glass and tossed mine back and she matched me, biting on the lime in the wake.

On the screen a man climbed in the rigging. Eve was getting loud: "The man holds a knife in his teeth while he risks death high above the deck." Eve was loud; several heads turned. "His fucking knife in his teeth."

I'd seen this; she wouldn't stop until there was trouble. She'd make a mess and end up crying and I'd hold her until she was certain I was miserable, my shirtfront wet, wrecked from her crying; we'd get in her car and there would be some kissing until she was absolutely certain that I was more miserable than she was, and then she'd get straight, sit up, be brave, and we'd part, promising to call. It was a friendship; it was that thing, the postcoital friendship, always hard to balance. We'd been lovers for three months two years ago. I had been in the process of getting married at the time, and it all had been a dangerous game. I mean, Eve knew I wasn't going to marry her. She came to the wedding and glowed there, wearing the occasion on her chest like a medal. I've known her for a long time and she never stood as tall as she did that day, her chin a lesson for the congregation and an inside joke for our office friends. She immediately started going with Christopher, also a joke, two careerists, doomed from the get-go. Now we did this: she called, we met, I took my medicine. The drinks had registered in me a little, but I was pretty sure I wanted it over now.

Errol Flynn was back on deck, his face wet, hurrying to organize the men on the ship, and I reached across Eve and took the remote and changed the channels until Arvell Larsen, the weather guy, popped up. She turned her head with great care toward me and said, "I wasn't going to make a scene. I was just happy to finally see a man with a knife in his mouth climbing the rigging. It's been a while." She lifted her glass and it seemed to light her face there; her clear, hand-some face was compelling. She had a kind of hard perfection wonderful on television. People who just met her always looked twice in the first minute. "Can you stay? We could order some food. You like the quesadilla, right?"

I looked at her. I like to look at people; I like the charged moments and Eve knew it, accused me of being addicted to them and thereby manipulative, coy, fake, an asshole. We had eye contact there, and anybody can say what they want to say, but eye contact is it, the beginning, middle, and end. It is bet-ter and worse, stronger than fondling in a hallway, stealing a kiss, better than any touch, and I held the look, feeling it work in me, glide, and then I reset myself and opened my mouth.

"You better not," she said. "Not that our gal Debbie has assumed an interest in cooking or learned to cook or even how to gather and prepare half a meal, but it will be dinnertime soon, and where is the new husband? Shall we picture her there in your bright new kitchen, standing at the ready as if to open the fridge: What is that worried look on her face? I'm being such a bitch here. Is she concerned about her mate or . . . Fuck it, Matt. This is just the way I talk. I like Debbie. You can't stay to eat. And me, what do I want to do, eat bar food with some man? Please, forget I said anything."

Our table already looked like the party was over—seven glasses, three bottles, two napkins, assorted silverware splayed around the ashtray, the plastic bib holding the drink specials on one side and the appetizers on the other. I began to line up the silverware. It had been an old game of ours to remove the card with the appetizer specials on it, fold it inside out and write notes, sayings, mine always being, "A thirsty man has nothing for tears." Now I just lined it up with the rest of the gear; I was lining things up. The late sun had dropped to the roadway and shot three powerhouse beams through the room, making the whole place only brown and gold, a science fiction scene, too bright, dangerous, throwing the shadows of the pool players against the far wall like storm clouds for a beat, and then a moment later as I finished my pathetic organizing of our tabletop, it all broke, the square girders of light dissipating into the bogus brown bar light, and we both looked up at our television for a moment, a woman identical to Eve with a microphone in front of an apartment building in New York. We couldn't hear what she was saying.

I took a drink of the Red Stripe. "I like the bottles as much as the beer," I said.

Eve leveled her look at me. "That's the way it is."

"The worst beer bottle?" I asked.

"Michelob," she said without hesitating. "Stupid. Designed for nothing. Looks like it should be full of children's shampoo."

I smiled. "You're sharp," I said.

"Don't," Eve said, pointing the television remote at my

chest, "you patronize me. You can leave anytime you want, but do not sit there and try to kiss my ass."

There was a cheer from the corner and the tall guy in a blue pinstripe shirt stood and raised his arms in a victory salute. Eve went on, "But this isn't a good idea, is it? Idle chatter. We were smart and good at it once, but it was because it led somewhere. We'd meet and fence and once you saw how bright I was again we'd go to bed. Now it is what it is: idle chatter." We watched the tall guy high-five his buddies, and Eve pointed. "There you are now. You had a couple of shirts like that; it's a good shirt for you, so blue, so noncommital."

Now I was ready to get out. The beer was good and I always liked the rush of being with Eve, being seen with her, but I wanted to leave, get back to my life. Eve pointed the remote at the tall young man, and I saw the channel change over there.

"Oh my God," Eve whispered.

"What did you do?" I asked her.

There was an uproar from his mates. One cried out, "What'd you do, Ted!" and Ted turned and opened his arms before them—*I'll take care of this*—and reached up to the elevated screen and put it back on the game. He turned and pointed at the guy who had complained, said something, and they all laughed.

"When you'd come to work in those shirts, I couldn't wait for you to take your jacket off, come by my desk." Eve wasn't looking at me. "They have a nice upper yoke, well made, and the cotton is satisfying to iron. The first time I saw that shirt, I knew you'd put it on the back of the rocker in my bedroom."

"I remember that chair."

"Don't remember it," she said. Again she touched the remote and we heard the group in the corner complain. Ted stood and reached up for the controls. He looked at something standing there in the corner of the dark brown room. Eve let him right the set and sit down before she did it again. Now several loud curses sounded, and Ted, of course, stood and tried to fix the problem. "Don't remember my furniture." The channels in the corner were spinning in a blur. "My furniture is not your concern, thank you, mister." Then there was tumult in the corner, one guy yelling out "What!" and also standing. "This is not a good idea!" he called to the room in general.

Eve looked at me. There were no tears there, and no gloating. "You think things happen and then they get to be good ideas later? Is that what we did? Dive in and then hope it was something even workable?" She stopped their television at a car commercial, some sleek vehicle on a winding wet country lane, an unreal place.

I told her the truth: "I wouldn't know an idea, Eve, let alone a good one. I wanted to sleep with you—anyone in this room would. Face it, you're a prize. You don't get to win. You get to be the prize." I touched her face, the skin there, knowing I could.

She stood up. It was an amazing thing, her standing next to me, so beautiful, her body in a green dress, her posture impeccable in the lost light. She pointed the remote at Ted's television now and held it like the beam that held the entire room hostage, and I felt it, like some cord that when it snapped would rock us all, and so I simply sat and let all my stupidity gather. Behind me in the big space, the pool balls nickered.

The young man Ted looked over at us, turned, a handsome figure in the dim light. He moved toward us with a kind of bounce in his step, a young guy in a pin-striped shirt, and he was angry, the look on his face was exactly *What the hell?* I'd already made up my mind that if there was a fight I would fight, and I knew what I would say afterward in the short term and the long term, and I was gladdened to be wrong, sitting there so wrong, waiting for this fine young man. Where had he been? I'd been waiting to meet this guy for a long time.

Disclaimer

This is a work of fiction, and any resemblance to actual events, locales, or persons, living or dead, is merely coincidental, except for the restaurant I call the Wild Chicken, which was a real place actually called the Blue Bird, a drive-in fast-food joint I always drove past on my way to Debbie Delucca's house. I always liked the Blue Bird, all the lights on late at night, because I knew that I was going to get a cheeseburger and a vanilla shake, so many of which I enjoyed with Debbie Delucca herself, or alone if I was driving back late from her house wrecked from all the couch time with her. The couch time I put in this book was real, too, as was the couch itself, a kind of overstuffed deal with Debbie's mother's big red and blue afghan on the back, a blanket that wanted to get caught in the gears and dragged into the evening's activities quietly and inextricably, a beautiful bold coverlet with a repeated pattern of red geese against a blue sky. Of course, the Blue Bird, which I have called the Wild Chicken, and where I stood so many midnights under the fluorescent lights picking red and blue threads out of my hair waiting for a cheeseburger and a vanilla shake, is now a Custom Tile Outlet, a place you can go if you want your fireplace to look like the one in any Hilton.

I also should add here that Debbie's house is real, based on her real house, a green-sided thing on the corner of Concord and Eighth South that had a long shallow porch where I stood so many nights that year whispering with Debbie, giving Mrs. Eisenhour across the street a little show, I guess, as we would stand some nights for an hour saying good-bye and *I love you* and *I can't believe I've met someone like you* and *That was dreamy in there on the couch, I love you so much* and other direct dialogue which I've used in the text absolutely verbatim, probably the easiest thing of all the things in this book to write because everything we said is alive within my head after all these years, things actually said on the chilly fall nights there on Concord as we twisted closer, so lost some nights that we'd wipe our moist noses on each other's necks under the huge munificent blessing of the ancient poplar tree in her front yard, a real tree that held up the sky for a half a mile in every direction, a giant that dumped its leaves in unending ten-ton squadrons that fall like some kind of perfect setting for us, a backdrop, a movie; if it could give up its ten million golden secrets, a blizzard of leaves, then we could be in love, a tree as gone as the house in which Debbie Delucca lived, under the blades for the interstate years ago, a tree we'll never any of us see again.

No coincidence is going to bring that tree back, nor Debbie Delucca, who was my close associate all those years, the young person with whom I invented modern love, love as we know it. Love which so many people dabble in today, but do not study or understand or allow to course through their veins like some necessary thing. We were the last people to use love right. She's now Debbie Delucca Peterson somewhere in St. Clare, where she does who knows what. I can't imagine, though I've tried. And what am I going to do, go into the ShopMart down there and run into her at the little lunch counter they've got over by the children's department as she sits quietly sipping some chicken noodle soup and reading this very book and nodding at how accurate every word is— the things she said, the things I said in return? And I'd sit down beside her and order a vanilla shake, not even wanting their fake version of one of the world's great treats, not even real ice cream, nor real vanilla, but wanting to say the words the way I did so many nights under the bright lights of the Blue Bird Cafe, *vanilla shake,* to see if she might turn to see who's talking like this, looking up from a book that I'm sorry now I even wrote, really sorry, because I see it for the first time: you can't get anything back. No coincidence at some lunch counter and twenty minutes of conversation with a girl you once knew, some woman sitting there, and you know the exact location of every mole on her body, is going to make one thing in this real world different. If you want the coincidence where some character based on me gets the amazing girl back and has his heart start again after so many years, you're going to have to look in a book.

II

THE ORDINARY SON

THE STORY OF MY FAMOUS family is a story of genius and its
consequences, I suppose, and I am uniquely and particularly
suited to tell the story since genius avoided me—and I it—
and I remain an ordinary man, if there is such a thing, calm
in all weathers, aware of event, but uninterested and generally incapable of deciphering implication. As my genius
brother Garrett used to say, "Reed, you're not screwed too
tight like the rest of us, but you're still screwed." Now, there's
a definition of the common man you can trust, and further,
you can trust me. There's no irony in that or deep inner
meaning or Freudian slips, any kind of slips really, simply
what it says. My mother told me many times I have a good
heart, and of course, she was a genius, and that heart should
help with this story, but a heart, as she said so often, good as it
may be, is always trouble.

Part of the reason this story hasn't come together before,
the story of my famous family, is that no one remembers they
were related. They all had their own names. My father was
Duncan Landers, the noted NASA physicist, the man respon-
sible for every facet of the photography of the first moon
landing. There is still camera gear on the moon inscribed
with this name. That is, Landers. He was born Duncan Lrsdyksz, which was changed when NASA began their public-

relations campaigns in the mid-sixties; the space agency suggested that physicists who worked for NASA should have more vowels in their names. They didn't want their press releases to seem full of typographical errors or foreigners. Congress was reading this stuff. So Lrsdyksz became Landers. (My father's close associate Igor Oeuroi didn't get just vowels; his name became LeRoy Rodgers. After le Cowboy Star, my mother quipped.)

My mother was Gloria Rainstrap, the poet who spent twenty years fighting for workers' rights from Texas to Alaska; in one string she gave four thousand consecutive lectures in her travels, not missing a night as she drove from village to village throughout the country. It still stands as some kind of record.

Wherever she went, she stirred up the best kind of trouble, reading her work and then spending hours in whatever guest house or spare bedroom she was given, reading the poems and essays of the people who had come to see her. She was tireless, driven by her overwhelming sense of fairness, and she was certainly the primary idealist to come out of twentieth-century Texas. When she started leaving home for months, years at a time, I was just a lad, but I remember her telling my father, Duncan, one night, "Texas is too small for what I have to do."

This was not around the dinner table. We were a family of geniuses and did not have a dinner table. In fact, the only table we did have was my father's drafting table, which was in the entry so that you had to squeeze sideways to even get into our house. "It sets the tone," Duncan used to say. "I want anyone coming into our home to see my work. That work is the reason we have a roof, anyway." He said that one day after my friend Jeff Shreckenbah and I inched past him on the way to my room. "And who are these people coming in the door?"

"It is your son and his friend," I told him.

"Good," he said, his benediction, but he said it deeply into his drawing, which is where he spent his time at home. He wouldn't have known if the Houston Oilers had arrived, because he was about to invent the modern gravity-free vacuum hinge that is still used today.

Most of my father, Duncan Landers's, work was classified, top-secret, eyes-only, but it didn't matter. No one except Jeff Shreckenbah came to our house. People didn't come over.

We were geniuses. We had no television, and we had no telephone. "What should I do," my father would say from where he sat in the entry, drawing, "answer some little buzzing device? Say hello to it?" NASA tried to install phones for us. Duncan took them out. It was a genius household and not to be diminished by primitive electronic foo-fahs.

My older sister was named Christina by my father and given the last name Rossetti by my mother. When she finally fled from M.I.T. at nineteen, she gave herself a new surname: Isotope. There had been some trouble, she told me, personal trouble, and she needed the new name to remind herself she wouldn't last long—and then she asked me how I liked my half-life. I was twelve then, and she laughed and said, "I'm kidding, Reed. You're not a genius; you're going to live forever." I was talking to her on the "hot line," the secret phone our housekeeper, Clovis Armandy, kept in a kitchen cupboard.

"Where are you going?" I asked her.

"West with Mother," she said. Evidently, Gloria Rainstrap had driven up to Boston to rescue Christina from some sort of meltdown. "A juncture of some kind," my father told me. "Not to worry."

Christina said, "I'm through with theoretical chemistry, but chemistry isn't through with me. Take care of Dad. See you later."

We three children were eight years apart; that's how geniuses plan their families. Christina had been gone for years, it seemed, from our genius household; she barely knew our baby brother, Garrett.

Garrett and I took everything in stride. We accepted that we were a family of geniuses and that we had no telephone or refrigerator or proper beds. We thought it was natural to eat crackers and sardines months on end. We thought the front yard was supposed to be a jungle of overgrown grass, weeds, and whatever reptiles would volunteer to live there. Twice a year the City of Houston street crew came by and mowed it all down, and daylight would pour in for a month or two. We had no cars. My father was always climbing into white Chevrolet station wagons, unmarked, and going off to the NASA Space Center south of town. My mother was always stepping up into orange VW buses driven by other people and driving off to tour. My sister had been the youngest student at M.I.T. My brother and I did our own laundry for years and walked to school, where by about seventh grade, we began to see the differences between the way ordinary people lived and the way geniuses lived. Other people's lives, we learned, centered fundamentally on two things: television and soft foods rich with all the versions of sugar.

By the time I entered junior high school, my mother's travels had kicked into high gear, and she hired a woman we came to know well, Clovis Armandy, to live in and to assist with our corporeal care. Gloria Rainstrap's parental theory and practice could be summed up by the verse I heard her say a thousand times before I reached the age of six: "Feed the soul, the body finds a way." And she fed our souls with a groaning banquet of iron ethics at every opportunity. She wasn't interested in sandwiches or casseroles. She was the kind of person who had a moral motive for her every move.

We had no refrigerator because it was simply the wrong way to prolong the value of food, which had little value in the first place. We had no real furniture because furniture became the numbing insulation of drones for the economy, an evil in itself. If religion was the opiate of the masses, then home furnishings were the Novocain of the middle class. Any small surfeit of comfort undermined our moral fabric. *We live for the work we can do, not for things,* she told us. I've met and heard lots of folks who shared Gloria's posture toward life on this earth, but I've never found anyone who put it so well, presented her ideas so convincingly, beautifully, and so insistently. They effectively seduced you into wanting to go without. I won't put any of her poems in this story, but they were transcendent. The *Times* called her "Buddha's angry daughter." My mother's response to people who were somewhat shocked at our empty house and its unkempt quality was, "We're ego distant. These little things," she'd say, waving her hand over the litter of the laundry, discarded draft paper, piles of top-secret documents in the hallway, various toys, the odd empty tin of sardines, "don't bother us in the least. We aren't even here for them." I always loved that last and still use it when a nuisance arises: I'm not even here for it. "Ego distant," my friend Jeff Shreckenbah used to say, standing in our empty house, "which means your ma doesn't sweat the small stuff."

My mother's quirk, and one she fostered, was writing on the bottom of things. She started it because she was always gone, away for months at a time, and she wanted us to get her messages throughout her absence and thereby be reminded again of making correct decisions and ethical choices. It was not unusual to find ballpoint-pen lettering on the bottom of our shoes, and little marker messages on the bottom of plates (where she wrote in a tiny script), and anywhere that you

could lift up and look under, she would have left her mark.
These notes primarily confused us. There I'd be in math class
and cross my legs and see something on the edge of my
sneaker and read, "Your troubles, if you stay alert, will pass
very quickly away."

I'm not complaining. I never, except once or twice, felt
deprived. I like sardines, still. It was a bit of a pinch when we
got to high school, and I noted with new poignancy that I
didn't quite have the wardrobe to keep up. Geniuses dress
plain but clean, and not always as clean as their ordinary
counterparts, who have nothing better to do with their lives
than buy and sort and wash clothes.

Things were fine. I turned seventeen. I was hanging out
sitting around my bare room, reading books, the History of
This, the History of That, dry stuff, waiting for my genius to
kick in. This is what had happened to Christina. One day
when she was ten, she was having a tea party with her dolls,
which were two rolled pink towels, the next day she cataloged
and diagrammed the amino acids, laying the groundwork for
two artificial sweeteners and a mood elevator. By the time my
mother, Gloria Rainstrap, returned from the Northwest and
my father looked up from his table, the State Department
"mentors" had been by and my sister, Christina, was on her
way to the inner sanctums of the Massachusetts Institute of
Technology. I remember my mother standing against my
father's drafting table, her hands along the top. Her jaw was
set and she said, "This is meaningful work for Christina, her
special doorway."

My father dragged his eyes up from his drawings and said,
"Where's Christina now?"

So the day I went into Garrett's room and found him writing equations on a huge scroll of butcher paper, which he had
used until that day to draw battle re-creations of the French

and Indian War, was a big day for me. I stood there in the gloom, watching him crawl along the paper, reeling out figures of which very few were numbers I recognized, most of the symbols being X's and Y's and the little twisted members of the Greek alphabet, and I knew that it had skipped me. Genius had cast its powerful, clear eye on me and said, "No thanks." At least I was that smart. I realized that I was not going to get to be a genius.

The message took my body a piece at a time, loosening each joint and muscle on the way up and then filling my face with a strange warmth, which I knew immediately was relief.

I was free.

I immediately took a job doing landscaping and general cleanup and maintenance at the San Jacinto Resort Motel on the old Hempstead Highway. My friend Jeff Shreckenbah worked next door at Alfredo's American Cafe, and he had told me that the last guy doing handiwork at the motel had been fired for making a holy mess of the parking lot with a paintbrush, and when I applied, Mr. Rakkerts, the short little guy who owned the place, took me on. These were the days of big changes for me. I bought a car, an act that would have at one time been as alien for me as intergalactic travel or applying to barber college. I bought a car. It was a four-door lime-green Plymouth Fury III, low miles. I bought a pair of chinos. These things gave me exquisite pleasure. I was seventeen and I had not known the tangible pleasure of having things. I bought three new shirts and a wristwatch with a leather strap, and I went driving in the evenings, alone south from our subdivision of Spring Woods with my arm on the green sill of my lime-green Plymouth Fury III through the vast spaghetti bowl of freeways and into the mysterious network of towers that was downtown Houston. It was my dawning.

Late at night, my blood rich with wonder at the possibilities of such a vast material planet, I would return to our tumbledown genius ranch house, my sister off putting new legs on the periodic table at M.I.T., my mother away in Shreveport showing the seaport workers there the way to political and personal power, my brother in his room edging closer to new theories of rocket reaction and thrust, my father sitting by the entry, rapt in his schematics. As I came in and sidled by his table and the one real light in the whole front part of the house, his pencilings on the space station hinge looking as beautiful and inscrutable to me as a sheet of music, he'd say my name as simple greeting. "Reed."

"Duncan," I'd say in return.

"How goes the metropolis?" he'd add, not looking up. His breath was faintly reminiscent of sardines; in fact, I still associate that smell, which is not as unpleasant as it might seem, with brilliance. I know he said *metropolis* because he didn't know for a moment which city we were in.

"It teems with industrious citizenry well into the night," I'd answer.

Then he'd say it, "Good," his benediction, as he'd carefully trace his lead-holder and its steel-like wafer of 5H pencil-lead along a precise new line deep into the vast white space. "That's good."

The San Jacinto Resort Motel along the Hempstead Highway was exactly what you might expect a twenty-unit motel to be in the year 1966. The many bright new interstates had come racing to Houston and collided downtown in a maze, and the old Hempstead Highway had been supplanted as a major artery into town. There was still a good deal of traffic on the four-lane, and the motel was always about half full, and as you would expect, never the same half. There were three permanent occupants, including a withered old man named Newcombe Shinetower, who was a hundred years old that summer and who had no car, just a room full of magazines with red and yellow covers, stacks of these things with titles like *Too Young for Comfort* and *Treasure Chest.* There were other titles. I was in Mr. Shinetower's room only on two occasions. He wore the same flannel shirt every day of his life and was heavily gone to seed. Once or twice a day I would see him shuffling out toward Alfredo's American Cafe, where Jeff told me he always ate the catfish. "You want to live to be a hundred," Jeff said, "eat the catfish." I told him I didn't know about a hundred and that I generally preferred smaller fish. I was never sure if Mr. Shinetower saw me or not as I moved through his line of sight. He might have nodded; it was hard to tell. What I felt was that he might exist on another plane, the way rocks are said to; they're in there but in a rhythm too slow for humans to perceive.

It was in his room, rife with the flaking detritus of the ages, that Jeff tried to help me reckon with the new world. "You're interested in sex, right?" he asked me one day as I took my break at the counter of Alfredo's. I told him I was, but that wasn't exactly the truth. I was indifferent. I understood how it was being packaged and sold to the American people, but it did not stir me, nor did any of the girls we went to school with, many of whom were outright beauties and not bashful about it. This was Texas in the sixties. Some of these buxom girls would grow up and try to assassinate their daughters' rivals on the cheerleading squad. If sex was the game, some seemed to say, deal me in. And I guess I felt it was a game, too, one I could sit out. I had begun to look a little closer at the ways I was different from my peers, worrying about anything that might be a genius tendency. And I took great comfort in the unmistakable affection I felt for my Plymouth Fury III.

"Good," he said. "If you're interested, then you're safe; you're not a genius. Geniuses"—here he leaned closer to me and squinted his eyes up to let me know this was a ground-breaking postulate—"have a little trouble in the sex department."

I liked Jeff; he was my first "buddy." I sat on the round red Naugahyde stool at Alfredo's long Formica counter and listened to his speech, including, "sex department," and I don't know, it kind of made sense to me. There must have been something on my face, which is a way of saying there must have been nothing on my face, absolutely nothing, a blank blank, because Jeff pulled his apron off his head and said, "Meet me out back in two minutes." He looked down the counter to where old Mr. Shinetower sucked on his soup. "We got to get you some useful information."

Out back, of course, Jeff led me directly around to the motel and Mr. Shinetower's room, which was not unlocked, but opened when Jeff gave the doorknob a healthy rattle. Inside in the sour dark, Jeff lit the lamp and picked up one of the old man's periodicals.

Jeff held the magazine and thumbed it like a deck of cards, stopping finally at a full-page photograph that he presented to me with an odd kind of certainty. "There," he said. "This is what everybody is trying for. This is the goal." It was a glossy color photograph, and I knew what it was right away, even in the poor light, a shiny shaved pubis, seven or eight times larger than life size. "This makes the world go round."

I was going along with Jeff all the way on this, but that comment begged for a remark, which I restrained. I could feel my father in me responding about the forces that actually caused and maintained the angular momentum of the earth. Instead I looked at the picture, which had its own lurid beauty. Of course, what it looked like was a landscape, a barren but promising promontory in not this but another world, the seam too perfect a fold for anything but ceremony. I imagined landing a small aircraft on the tawny slopes and approaching the entry, stepping lightly with a small party of explorers, alert for the meaning of such a place. The air would be devoid of the usual climatic markers (no clouds or air pressure), and in the stillness we would be silent and reverential. The light in the photograph captivated me in that it seemed to come from everywhere, a flat, even twilight that would indicate a world with one or maybe two distant polar suns. There was an alluring blue shadow that ran along the cleft the way a footprint in snow holds its own blue glow, and that aberration affected and intrigued me.

Jeff had left my side and was at the window, on guard, pleased that I was involved in my studies. "So," he said. "It's really something, isn't it?" He came to me, took the magazine and took one long look at the page the way a thirsty man drinks from a jug, and he set it back on the stack of Old Man Shinetower's magazines.

"Yes," I said. "It certainly is." Now that it was gone, I realized I had memorized the photograph, that place.

"Come on. Let's get out of here before he gets back." Jeff cracked the door and looked out, both ways. "Whoa," he said, setting the door closed again. "He's coming back. He's on the walk down about three rooms." Jeff then did an amazing thing: he dropped like a rock to all fours and then onto his stomach and slid under the bed. I'd never seen anyone do that; I've never seen it since. I heard him hiss: "Do something. Hide."

Again I saw myself arriving in the photograph. Now I was alone. I landed carefully and the entire venture was full of care, as if I didn't want to wake something. I had a case of instruments and I wanted to know about that light, that shadow. I could feel my legs burn as I climbed toward it step by step.

What I did in the room was take two steps back into the corner and stand behind the lamp. I put my hands at my side and my chin up. I stood still. At that moment we heard a key in the lock and daylight spilled across the ratty shag carpet. Mr. Shinetower came in. He was wearing the red-and-black plaid shirt that he wore every day. It was like a living thing; someday it would go to lunch at Alfredo's without him.

He walked by me and stopped for a moment in front of the television to drop a handful of change from his pocket into a mason jar on top, turn on the television until it lit and focused, and then he continued into the little green bathroom, and I saw the door swing halfway closed behind him.

Jeff slid out from the bed, stood hastily, his eyes whirling, and opened the door and went out. He was closing it behind him when I caught the edge and followed him into the spinning daylight. When I pulled the door, he gasped, so I shut it and we heard it register closed, and then we slipped quickly through the arbor to the alley behind the units and then ran along the overgrown trail back to the bayou and sat on the weedy slope. Jeff was covered with clots of dust and hairy white goo-gah. It was thick in his hair and I moved away from him while he swatted at it for a while. Here we could smell the sewer working at the bayou, an odd, rich industrial silage, and the sky was gray, but too bright to look at, and I went back to the other world for a moment, the cool perfect place I'd been touring in Mr. Shinetower's magazine, quiet and still, and offering that light. Jeff was spitting and pulling feathers of dust from his collar and sleeves. I wanted so much to be stirred by what I had seen; I had stared at it and I wanted it to stir me, and it had done something. I felt something. I wanted to see that terrain, chart it, understand where the blue glow arose and how it lay along the juncture, and how that light, I was certain, interfered with the ordinary passage of time. Time? I had a faint headache.

"That was close," Jeff said finally. He was still cloaked with flotsam from under Mr. Shinetower's bed. "But it was worth it. Did you get a good look? See what I'm talking about?"

"It was a remarkable photograph," I said.

"Now you know. You've seen it, you know. I've got to get back to work. Let's go fishing this weekend, eh?" He rose and, still whacking soot and ashes and wicked whatevers from his person, ran off toward Alfredo's.

"I've seen it," I said, and I sat there as the sadness bled through me. Duncan would have appreciated the moment and corrected Jeff the way he corrected me all those years. "Seeing isn't knowing," he would say. "To see something is only to establish the first terms of your misunderstanding." That I remembered him at such a time above the rife bayou moments after my flight over the naked photograph made me sad. I was not a genius, but I would be advised by one forevermore.

Happily, my work at the motel was straightforward and I enjoyed it very much. I could do most of it with my shirt off, cutting away the tenacious vines from behind each of the rooms so that the air-conditioning units would not get strangled, and I sweated profusely in the sweet humid air. I painted the pool fence and enameled the three metal tables a kind of turquoise blue, a fifties turquoise that has become tony again just this year, a color that calls to the passerby: Holiday! We're on holiday!

Once a week I poured a pernicious quantity of lime into the two manholes above the storm sewer, and it fell like snow on the teeming backs of thousands of albino waterbugs and roaches that lived there. This did not daunt them in the least. I am no expert on any of the insect tribes nor do I fully understand their customs, but my association with those subterranean multitudes showed me that they looked forward to this weekly toxic snowfall.

Twice a week I pressed the enormous push broom from one end of the driveway to the other until I had a wheelbarrow full of gravel and the million crushed tickets of litter people threw from their moving vehicles along the Hempstead Highway. It was wonderful work. The broom alone weighed twenty pounds. The sweeping, the painting, the trimming braced me; work that required simply my back, both my arms and both my legs, but neither side of my brain.

Mr. Leeland Rakkerts lived in a small apartment behind the office and could be summoned by a bell during the night hours. He was just sixty that June. His wife had passed away years before and he'd become a reclusive little gun nut, and had a growing gallery of hardware on a pegboard in his apartment featuring long-barreled automatic weaponry and at least two dozen huge handguns. But he was fine to me, and he paid me cash every Friday afternoon. When he opened the cash drawer, he always made sure that be you friend or foe, you saw the .45 pistol that rested there, too. My mother would have abhorred me working for him, a man she would have considered the enemy, and she would have said as much, but I wasn't taking the high road, nor the low road, just a road. That summer, the upkeep of the motel was my job, and I did it as well as I could. I'd taken a summer job and was making money. I didn't weigh things on my scale of ethics every ten minutes, because I wasn't entirely sure I had such a scale. I certainly didn't have one as fully evolved as my mother's.

It was a bit like being in the army: when in doubt, paint something. I remeasured and overpainted the parking lot where the last guy had drunkenly painted a wacky series of parentheses where people were supposed to park, and I did a good job with a big brush and five gallons of high mustard yellow, and when I finished I took the feeling of satisfaction in my chest to be simply that: satisfaction. Even if I was working for the devil, the people who put their cars in his parking lot would be squared away.

Getting in my Plymouth Fury III those days with a sweaty back and a pocketful of cash, I knew I was no genius, but I felt—is this close? —like a great guy, a person of some command.

That fall my brother, Garrett Lrsdyksz (he'd changed his name back with a legal kit that Baxter, our Secret Service guy, had got him through the mail), became the youngest student to matriculate at Rice University. He was almost eleven. And he didn't enter as a freshman; he entered as a junior. In physics, of course. There was a little article about it on the wire services, noting that he had, without any assistance, set forward the complete set of equations explaining the relationship between the rotation of the earth and "special atmospheric aberrations most hospitable to exit trajectories of ground-fired propulsion devices." You can look it up and all you'll find is the title because the rest, like all the work he did his cataclysmic year at Rice, is classified, top-secret, eyes-only. Later he explained his research this way to me: "There are storms and then there are storms, Reed. A high-pressure area is only a high-pressure area down here on earth; it has a different pressure on the other side."

I looked at my little brother, a person forever in need of a haircut, and I thought: He's mastered the other side, and I can just barely cope with this one.

That wasn't exactly true, of course, because my Plymouth Fury III and my weekly wages from the San Jacinto Resort

Motel allowed me to start having a little life, earthbound as it may have been. I started hanging out a little at Jeff Shrecken-bah's place, a rambling hacienda out of town with two out-buildings where his dad worked on stock cars. Jeff's mother called me Ladykiller, which I liked, but which I couldn't hear without imagining my mother's response; my mother who told me a million times, "Morality commences in the words we use to speak of our next act."

"Hey, Ladykiller," Mrs. Shreckenbah would say to me as we pried open the fridge looking for whatever we could find. Mr. Shreckenbah made me call him Jake, saying we'd save the last names for the use of the law-enforcement officials and members of the Supreme Court. They'd let us have Lone Star long-necks if we were staying, or Coca-Cola if we were hit-ting the road. Some nights we'd go out with Jake and hand him wrenches while he worked on his cars. He was always asking me, "What's the plan?" an opening my mother would have approved of.

"We're going fishing," I told him, because that's what Jeff and I started doing. I'd greet his parents, pick him up, and then Jeff and I would cruise hard down Interstate 45 fifty miles to Galveston and the coast of the warm Gulf of Mexico, where we'd drink Lone Star and surf-cast all night long, haul-ing in all sorts of mysteries of the deep. I loved it.

Jeff would bring along a pack of Dutch Masters cigars and I'd stand waist deep in the warm water, puffing on the cheap cigar, throwing a live shrimp on a hook as far as I could toward the equator, the only light being the stars above us, the gapped two-story skyline of Galveston behind us, and our bonfire on the beach, tearing a bright hole in the world.

When fish struck, they struck hard, waking me from vivid daydreams of Mr. Leeland Rakkerts giving me a bonus for sweeping the driveway so thoroughly, a twenty so crisp it hurt to fold it into my pocket. My dreams were full of crisp twenties. I could see Jeff over there, fifty yards from me, the little orange tip of his cigar glowing, starlight on the flash of his line as he cast. I liked having my feet firmly on the bottom of the ocean standing in the night. My brother and sister and my mother and father could shine their lights into the elemental mysteries of the world; I could stand in the dark and fish. I could feel the muscles in my arm as I cast again; I was stronger than I'd been two months ago, and then I felt the fish strike and begin to run south.

Having relinquished the cerebral, not that I ever had it in my grasp, I was immersing myself in the real world the same way I was stepping deeper and deeper into the Gulf, following the frenzied fish as he tried to take my line. I worked him back, gave him some, worked him back. Though I had no idea what I would do with it, I had decided to make a lot of money, and as the fish drew me up to my armpits and the bottom grew irregular, I thought about the ways it might be achieved. Being no genius, I had few ideas.

I spit out my cigar after the first wavelet broke over my face, and I called to Jeff, "I got one."

He was behind me now, backing toward the fire, and he called, "Bring him up here and let's see."

The top half of my head, including my nose, and my two hands and the fishing pole were all that were above sea level when the fish relented and I began to haul him back. He broke the surface several times as I backed out of the ocean, reeling as I went. Knee deep, I stopped and lifted the line until a dark form lifted into the air. I ran him up to Jeff by the fire and showed him there, a two-pound catfish. When I held him, I felt the sudden shock of his gaffs going into my finger and palm.

"Ow!" Jeff said. "Who has got whom?" He took the fish from me on a gill stick.

I shook my stinging hand.

"It's all right," he assured me, throwing another elbow of driftwood onto the fire and handing me an icy Lone Star. "Let's fry this guy up and eat him right now. I'm serious. This is going to be worth it. We're going to live to be one hundred years old, guaranteed."

We'd sit, eat, fish some more, talk, and late late we'd drive back, the dawn light gray across the huge tidal plain, smoking Dutch Masters until I was queasy and quiet, dreaming about my money, however I would make it.

Usually this dream was interrupted by my actual boss, Mr. Leeland Rakkerts, shaking my shoulder as I stood sleeping on my broom in the parking lot of the hot and bothered San Jacinto Resort Motel, saying, "Boy! Hey! Boy! You can take your zombie fits home or get on the stick here." I'd give him the wide-eyed nod and continue sweeping, pushing a thousand pounds of scraggly gravel into a conical pile and hauling it in my wheelbarrow way out back into the thick tropical weeds at the edge of the bayou and dumping it there like a body. It wasn't a crisp twenty-dollar bill he'd given me, but it was a valuable bit of advice for a seventeen-year-old, and I tried to take it as such.

Those Saturdays after we'd been to the Gulf beat in my skull like a drum, the Texas sun a thick pressure on my bare back as I moved through the heavy humid air skimming and vacuuming the pool, rearranging the pool furniture though it was never, ever moved because no one ever used the pool. People hadn't come to the San Jacinto Resort Motel to swim. Then standing in the slim shade behind the office, trembling under a sheen of sweat, I would suck on a tall bottle of Coca-Cola as if on the very nectar of life, and by midafternoon as I trimmed the hedges along the walks and raked and swept, the day would come back to me, a pure pleasure, my lime-green Plymouth Fury III parked in the shady side of Alfredo's American Cafe, standing like a promise of every sweet thing life could offer.

These were the days when my brother, Garrett, was coming home on weekends, dropped at our curb by the maroon Rice University van after a week in the research dorms, where young geniuses from all over the world lived in bare little cubicles, the kind of thing somebody with an I.Q. of 250 apparently loves. I had been to Garrett's room on campus and it was perfect for him. There was a kind of pad in one corner surrounded by a little bank of his clothing and the strip of butcher paper running the length of the floor, covered with numbers and letters and tracked thoroughly with the faint gray intersecting grid of sneaker prints. His window looked out onto the pretty green grass quad.

It was the quietest building I have ever been in, and I was almost convinced that Garrett might be the only inmate, but when we left to go down to the cafeteria for a sandwich, I saw the other geniuses in their rooms, lying on their stomachs like kids drawing with crayons on a rainy day. Then I realized that they were kids and it was a rainy day and they were working with crayons; the only difference was that they were drawing formulas for how many muons could dance on a quark.

Downstairs there were a whole slug of the little people in the dining hall sitting around in the plastic chairs, swinging their feet back and forth six inches off the floor, ignoring their trays of tuna-fish sandwiches and tomato soup, staring this way and then that as the idea storms in their brains swept through. You could almost see they were thinking by how their hair stood in fierce clusters.

There was one adult present, a guy in a blue sweater vest who went from table to table urging the children to eat: Finish that sandwich, drink your milk, go ahead, use your spoon, try the soup, it's good for you. I noticed he was careful to register and gather any of the random jottings the children committed while they sat around doodling in spilled milk. I guess he was a member of the faculty. It would be a shame for some nine-year-old to write the key to universal field theory in peanut butter and jelly and then eat the thing.

"So," I said as we sat down, "Garrett. How's it going?"

Garrett looked at me, his trance interrupted, and as it melted away and he saw me and the platters of cafeteria food before us, he smiled. There he was, my little brother, a sleepy-looking kid with a spray of freckles up and over his nose like the crab nebula, and two enthusiastic front teeth that would be keeping his mouth open for decades. "Reed," he said. "*How's it going?* I love that. I've always liked your acute sense of narrative. So linear and right for you." His smile, which took a moment and some force to assemble, was ancient, beneficent, as if he both envied and pitied me for something, and he shook his head softly. "But things here aren't going, kid." He poked a finger into the white bread of his tuna sandwich and studied the indentation like a man finding a footprint on the moon. "Things here *are*. This is it. Things . . ." He started again. "Things aren't bad, really. It's kind of a floating circle. That's close. Things aren't going; they float in the circle. Right?"

We were both staring at the sandwich; I think I might have been waiting for it to float, but only for a second. I understood what he was saying. Things existed. I'm not that dumb. Things, whatever they might be, and that was a topic I didn't even want to open, had essence, not process. That's simple; that doesn't take a genius to decipher. "Great," I said. And then I said what you say to your little brother when he sits there pale and distracted and four years ahead of you in school, "Why don't you eat some of that, and I'll take you out and show you my car."

It wasn't as bad a visit as I'm making it sound. We were brothers; we loved each other. We didn't have to say it. The dining room got me a little until I realized I should stop worrying about these children and whether or not they were happy. Happiness wasn't an issue. The place was clean; the food was fresh. Happiness, in that cafeteria, was simply beside the point.

On the way out, Garrett introduced me to his friend Donna Li, a ten-year-old from New Orleans, whom he said was into programming. She was a tall girl with shiny hair and a ready smile, eating alone by the window. This was 1966 and I was certain she was involved somehow in television. You didn't hear the word *computer* every other sentence back then. When she stood to shake my hand, I had no idea of what to say to her and it came out, "I hope your programming is floating in the circle."

"It is," she said.

"She's written her own language," Garrett assured me, "and now she's on the applications."

It was my turn to speak again and already I couldn't touch bottom, so I said, "We're going out to see my car. Do you want to see my car?"

Imagine me in the parking lot then with these two little kids. On the way out I'd told Garrett about my job at the motel and that Jeff Shreckenbah and I had been hanging out and fishing on the weekends and that Jeff's dad raced stock cars, and for the first time all day Garrett's face filled with a kind of wonder, as if this were news from another world, which I guess it was. There was a misty rain with a faint petrochemical smell in it, and we approached my car as if it were a sleeping Brontosaurus. They were both entranced and moved toward it carefully, finally putting their little hands on the wet fender in unison. "This is your car," Garrett said, and I wasn't sure if it was the *your* or the *car* that had him in awe.

I couldn't figure out what floats in the circle or even where the circle was, but I could rattle my keys and start that Plymouth Fury III and listen to the steady sound of the engine, which I did for them now. They both backed away appreciatively.

"It's a large car," Donna Li said.

"Reed," Garrett said to me. "This is really something. And what's that smell?"

I cocked my head, smelling it, too, a big smell, budging the petrocarbons away, a live, salty smell, and then I remembered: I'd left half a bucket of bait shrimp in the trunk, where they'd been ripening for three days since my last trip to Galveston with Jeff.

"That's rain in the bayou, Garrett."

"Something organic," Donna Li said, moving toward the rear of the vehicle.

"Here, guys," I said, handing Garrett the bag of candy, sardine tins, and peanut-butter-and-cheese packs I'd brought him. I considered for half a second showing him the pile of rotting crustaceans; it would have been cool and he was my brother. But I didn't want to give the geniuses the wrong first impression of the Plymouth.

"Good luck with your programming," I told Donna Li, shaking her hand. "And Garrett, be kind to your rocketry."

Garrett smiled at that again and said to Donna, "He's my brother."

And she added, "And he owns the largest car in Texas."

I felt bad driving my stinking car away from the two young

people, but it was that or fess up. I could see them standing in my rearview mirror for a long time. First they watched me, then they looked up, both of them for a long time. They were geniuses looking into the rain; I counted on their being able to find a way out of it.

EVIL EYE ALLEN

JANEY MORROW WAS A GIRL who possessed unparalleled beauty, a beauty that stood out like a beacon, the kind of beacon that warns ships of danger, a powerful thing that, though it is intended to serve some greater purpose, inevitably draws attention to itself. I haven't said that very well, but I tried to go that route because even to try to set out her features would be ridiculous. She was beautiful in a transcendent, unconventional way, and with such vitality and force that you knew—I did—not to look at her, her chinbone, the dark hair of her eyebrows as they flared, the arch of her mouth, any of it, because to look into or upon or near her bright, brooding, large-eyed face would seize you with a gravity you couldn't even begin to understand or contend with, and you would be unable to look away, even as the bell rang ending your trigonometry class. And as the eleventh-grade students zipped their backpacks and rose to leave, you would be bound and frozen there to stare at Janey Morrow's perfect, hyperperfect, superperfect face.

There was a relief in all of this in that even at seventeen I knew she wasn't a girl I was going to have to talk to, ever. I could see her, sense the glow of her aura, but I would never talk to her. It was okay with me. She was in my trigonometry class and I was able to hear Mr. Trachtenberg say her name three or four times every class period, for she was unparalleled also in her understanding of trigonometry.

I was having some trouble in trigonometry even before the real trouble that I will get to by and by, and I needed trigonometry to get into Dickinson College, which was my modest dream. I had heard of a writer there, a woman who actually let her students write stories and then talked to the students about this work, and that is what I wanted to do. To get into Dickinson I needed to pass trigonometry and I needed thousands of dollars. I started assisting Evil Eye Allen to solve the latter, but the power of his evil eye did something to assist me in the former as well.

My close friend Evil Eye Allen instructed me on more than one occasion as we reclined on the football bleachers that when I finally arrived at the story of his name, I must tell it truly yet with some delicacy. "Delicacy is absolutely underrated, Rick," he told me. "Delicacy is a kind of care the real truth requires." We were old friends by then, seventeen, everyone else having given us up as strange, me already known as a guy with notebooks, and Evil Eye, who never recovered from giving himself that name and never wanted to. It made me smile and remember his credo: Posture is message. Part of the reason he was considered too odd for friends was the way he had of posting his body when we sat or walked. He'd look straight up when he spoke to you or answer questions in class with his chin on his chest and his hand on the top of his head. "They'll remember your body," he said to me, "and then what you said. It's pivotal to use the body." He walked sideways or drifted backward. His hands were always in the air.

I remember his head, which bore his own self-administered haircut, a close, uneven job that made him look like someone in radical recovery, turning slowly, rolling like a machine part and clicking into place, focused right on me there high above the football field. "When you write the story of my name," Evil Eye Allen said to me, his voice now an airy whisper, "write the story truly but with delicacy. You're capable of that; you were there and you know me, and we've got to think of Janey. See what I mean?"

"I guess," I said.

"That would be the wrong answer," he said, folding up and realigning himself along the bench. "Leave nothing out. Put everything in the story; put all about Evil Eye and his assistant, but don't change the names. And put in Janey Morrow's election speech." His hand rose into the sky as if lifted by a string. "Word for word."

His name, of course, was not Evil Eye. His real name was Gary, and it would be great to start with something like *He was always a strange kid*, but that isn't true. He grew up two houses down from me and we were friends from day one, that is before we went to school, and he was a regular kid, better at chess than I, worse at poker, better at baseball, as good with football, liked by his teachers, my parents, girls. By the time we entered high school, he could have gone with any girl he wanted; he was real and kind and he had something else, an actor's magnetism and what I called poise.

"Poise," he'd say. "Please. Poise is never looking at your hands. I'm a bit beyond that. I'm using my body for something I don't even understand."

And so he got this reputation for being different, but it was an enviable different, something we would have imitated if we could have gotten ahold of it. Sometimes it was his elegant walk, sometimes the way his head seemed to be doing different work than his body, sometimes his mouth opening as he listened or offered you a quick smile. Here I was, a teenager, trying to walk straight, not collapse over my new size-twelve feet, and keep my shirt tucked in, and walking with me was this person who embodied grace, a person like I've never seen since, who used every step he took to do two if not three things. "Why do we go up the stairs?" he said to me one day that first year at Orkney High.

"Because we have language arts in 202," I told him, lugging my books up behind him.

"Rick. Oh, Rick. This would be the wrong answer," he said, a phrase I knew by heart. "We are communicating."

"Are we going up to language arts?" I asked.

"If that happens," he said, "so be it. But we are moving upward to say something to the ages." His right hand was clamped on the top of his head and his left under his chin, his hands free because he had given his books to me. "I'm glad you're here to see this." It's what he said later that year when he went a week without closing his mouth and when he went two days, school days, without speaking. That time he told me, "You don't need to talk. It's a luxury. Listen to me right now; I'm enjoying this, but I don't need to do it."

In February of that year, a certain girl came into Evil Eye's sights, a girl everyone else had already seen in that she was the most beautiful girl on dry land anywhere, a girl who was so popular and confident and finished, she seemed already above it all, a girl renowned for her snobbery and style, who every good soul in our school knew not to greet because there would be no greeting in return. She was self-contained, sealed shut with her abundant talents, and moving on a straight, graceful line through high school like a first-class car on the express rail. Her name was Janey Morrow. Evil Eye Allen was astounded at her carriage, her posture, her every manner, and he made it his mission to *cross into her perimeter*. Those are his words, not mine.

He began speaking to her. It was a picture: my tall friend standing on one leg or leaning his forehead against the wall by her locker as she did everything she could with her shoulder, books, and hands to let him know he should *go away now*.

"She has never once looked at me, made eye contact, or spoken in a complete sentence," he told me after the first week. "I don't mean even once, and it has been nine days. Is that magnificent or what?" He brought his hands up in a ball, squeezing his fists together and then springing them open. "She is *there*. She is together. We're not going to see something like this again." Now he took my shirt in both of his gigantic hands and whispered along the side of my face, "I'm going to get to her. Evil Eye Allen is going to *humanize* this angel."

In trigonometry, my teacher, Mr. Trachtenberg, bathed Miss Morrow, as he called her, in the soft fostering light of his appreciation. He assumed a stark hostility toward me. I needed a B; it said so in my college application. Trachtenberg had heard that I was Evil Eye Allen's assistant, and he was a man who was going to single-handedly use trigonometry to turn around the foolishness that was eroding the decade.

He discovered my alter ego as a result of our first flyer. We had produced a red-and-black announcement that offered the services of:

Evil Eye Allen and his able assistant, Igor, for Parties of Every Kind and Magnitude including Wedding Receptions, Bar Mitzvahs, Fertility Rites, Seances, Exorcisms, Arbor Day Festivities, Presidents' Day Celebrations, and Any Occasion Where Something Strange and the Presence of Mysterious Objects Would Make a Worthy Contribution and Amplify the Pleasure of Your Friends. "Beware the Power of the Evil Eye." Reasonable Rates.

Mr. Trachtenberg peeled one of these bold goodies off his classroom floor and was not amused to read what appeared to him to be a handbill from the devil. Mr. Trachtenberg's Christianity was famous. His religious zeal protruded from every axiom he scratched on the blackboard. "It is mathematics," he'd say, "which will finally defeat Satan." Last year a kid named Kenny Albright had quipped, "Well then, Mr. T., which is better against the devil, a crucifix or the quadratic equation?" Mr. Trachtenberg stopped at the board, frozen for ten complete seconds it was said, and then he turned, his black eyebrows already crashing together over his flashing eyes, and he whispered through his gnashing teeth, "Neither is going to save you, Mr. Albright." Kenny Albright, who was a sophomore about to be sixteen, started crying. He transferred into consumer math.

What Evil Eye hadn't told me, his able assistant, was that Mr. Trachtenberg's first name was Igor. And Mr. Trachtenberg made it clear, very clear, that there was room for only one Igor in fourth-period trigonometry. "Is this amusing, Mr. Wesson?" he asked me, waving the flyer before the class. "This, this appeal to the puerile, the ungodly, the evil? Is it?" He wasn't really asking, and he had the class's attention. Everyone was waiting to see if I was going to cry. I needed trig; consumer math wasn't going to get me into college. "I haven't seen the mark of the beast in your work. It's been haphazard and a bit tentative but not flagitious or depraved. Are you depraved, Mr. Wesson? Or is it *Igor?* Do you think in the hot center of your logical mind, Mr. Igor Wesson, that it would be a good idea for the impotent ant to mock the iron heel of my boot?"

No one moved. Everyone had heard that word, *impotent.* Everyone was waiting for me to gasp and begin sobbing. And the gasp was right there in my throat waiting to break. I could feel the impeccable presence of Janey Morrow at the desk next to mine. I steadied myself and spoke. "No, sir. It would be a bad idea to mock . . ." I could not go on.

"What, Mr. Wesson?"

"I need this class, Mr. Trachtenberg," I whispered. The edges of a hot tear seared the rim of my eye.

"Well, Igor. We'll see how badly you need it." He turned to the board. And so began the hardest ride in mathematics in the history of Orkney High School. I received that afternoon from the hand of Mr. Trachtenberg the supplemental text I would complete before June, a thick maroon hardback called *Advanced Concepts in Trigonometry*.

Evil Eye and I had several jobs right after our flyer appeared—house parties, a birthday—and after we did the half-hour intermission at the junior prom, our calendar filled into the summer. Suddenly, for the first time since my paper route, there was money; we charged forty dollars and then fifty (and there were tips). When Evil Eye would hand me my half, he'd say, "You're going to college."

Our act opened with me coming out in my red vest and white dress shirt buttoned to the collar, setting up our card table and covering it with a black tablecloth. Then I would light the fat black candle in the center and place the Mysterious Objects around it, showing each object to the crowd first. I would hold up some aviator sunglasses and set them down, a pink plastic shoehorn, a bucket handle, a pair of brass doorknobs. Sometimes there were other objects.

"What are these for?" I asked him the first time we practiced.

"These are the Mysterious Objects."

"What are the Mysterious Objects for?"

"That's right." He was busy tugging at the sleeves of his cape. It was an old graduation robe he'd found at the thrift shop and then gone at with a pair of pinking shears. "They're Mysterious Objects, which means there is no answer to your earnest question. The Objects have mystery."

"Do you know the mystery? I thought you got these things down at the Salvation Army."

Here he stopped hauling at the heavy garment and turned to me. "Mystery," he said. "Mystery." He wanted the word to be its own explanation. When I just looked at him dumb as the doorknob before us, he went on. "Igor. There are things beyond our knowing." He rolled his head in a big slow circle and brought it back to bear on me: "Do you know what we're doing?"

"No," I said.

Evil Eye crouched down and then rose onto his toes, framing his face in his hands, to announce: "I don't either." He put one hand over his eyes and waved the other in the air. "Do you think the unknown has power?"

"I guess," I said.

"Then," he said, looking at me, his hands now on guard for everything, "this room is full of power, because I don't know what any of this junk means, either. We're going to put on a show and try to find some things out!"

I sat down on the couch. "All I have to do is put out the stuff and stand behind you and hand you something if you need it, right?"

"Right. That and look worried. Look worried all the time."

Well, that wasn't hard. I was worried all the time. I was worried about Mr. Igor Trachtenberg and passing trigonometry, and thereby high school; I was worried about getting admitted to college and how I would afford it; I was worried about something else, some unnamed thing, which hovers about me still as a worrying person, and I was particularly worried twice a week about wearing a red vest over my long-sleeved white oxford cloth dress shirt and placing the Mysterious Objects on a card table in front of thirty people in somebody's living room.

The house parties were the worst for worry, because every one was so close. At the junior prom, for which we received two hundred dollars, there were four hundred people and I couldn't see one of them out there in the dark. I stood at the edge of the spotlight, set out the Mysterious Objects, and looked worried the whole time, but it was easier than standing in front of eighteen people in Eddie Noble's living room or Harriet Middleton's den. But to Evil Eye it was all the same. It didn't matter. He didn't have to set out the Mysterious Objects and then look worried. He had to come out in his hefty gown and wait until the audience, big or small, grew nervous, tittered, and then after a good long dose of silence, he would begin with his routine for the Evil Eye.

"Ladies and gentlemen," he would start. "No one here, not you, not me, not my able assistant Igor, knows what the next few minutes will bring. Do you understand? No one knows what is about to happen. I'm serious." With that sentence, *I'm serious*, he could make everyone sit up a little; it was clear that he meant it. "I," he'd continue, "am sometimes called the Evil Eye, because of what my look can engender . . ." And then it would all begin. He would cruise, drift, float the perimeter of the stage whether it was a forty-foot circle, as it was at the junior prom, or the width of three folding chairs, as it was at Harriet Middleton's birthday party. From where I stood I always saw the audience sit up and grow still and then imperceptibly at first begin to sway with Evil Eye as he floated, drifted, cruised back and forth before them. When he would stab a foot down and stop and stand straight up like a snake about to strike, I could see the audience sit up, lean back, prepare for the worst. He'd hop backward sometimes and I could see heads bob; and when he spun, everyone flinched; and when he stopped, the shadow of the spell was spilled over us all.

When the room was changed that way, sometimes a boy or

sometimes a girl would rise and step forward, standing by the Mysterious Objects, and then the rest would happen in a flurry. Evil Eye would hand them one of the Mysterious Objects, the doorknobs, or the sunglasses, and make a request: "What do you feel?" or "Tell us what it's like." And that was really it. Just the picture of the two of them—some stunned boy standing there in a madras shirt with Evil Eye in his monstrous robe—was the climax of the act. Everyone would be leaning forward. And when the boy said, "I'm glad I got my car running," or "This is weird," or "I can be scared and happy at the same time," it would have taken on a layer of danger and importance that made it amazing, and that's what people were really, *amazed*, and they applauded wildly and the subject would sit down and as the evening was retold in the weeks to come, the things the subject said would grow into dire predictions and ponderous epigrams, which only magnified Evil Eye's reputation. After every show, more kids called him Evil Eye, but his name was not carved in stone yet.

Mr. Igor Trachtenberg, the only thing between me and college, continued to try to drum me out of trig. I was doing double assignments anyway, our homework *and* ongoing chapters in *Advanced Concepts in Trigonometry,* and he would hand back my papers with a little pencil check at the bottom. A check. When I asked him what it meant, he said, "Are you still roving about doing the devil's handiwork?"

"No, sir," I told him, because I'm fairly sure that was the only answer to that question. "I'm doing problems in trigonometry three hours every night. I'm keeping the devil at bay."

Mr. Trachtenberg looked at me, his eyebrows in a dark, threatening arch. "I'll be the judge of that." Then he took my paper and drew a quick circle around the check and put two lines under that and handed my homework back to me. That was all the explanation I was going to get. Check, circle, underlines. It looked like his secret code for F. It looked like an evil eye.

Then Janey Morrow's dad called. "I didn't even know she had a dad," Evil Eye told me. "He wants to give Janey a birthday party."

"I hope this isn't anything but a nice birthday party for the most beautiful girl either of us will ever see on earth," I said.

"Meaning?"

"I hope this isn't some special way of incinerating two teenage idiots in a fire of their own design. I hope she's not out to get us."

"I am Evil Eye," he said to me. "It's way too late to get me, and you're a writer, so you're always safe."

Regardless, now charging eighty dollars for parties, we went out to Janey Morrow's for her seventeenth birthday party, the party that became the most retold of all of Evil Eye's outings, and the one that gave him his name once and for all because something else happened there that was permanent. If everyone who has told of the night at the little house on Concord Lane had actually been there, it would have been by far our largest crowd, but in fact there were only a dozen people. These were all the kids from school who distinguished themselves by knowing how to dress and knowing the first names of the faculty. I mean, one of the guys wore a sweater vest. These were kids who when they put their hands in the pockets of their slacks to lean against a cornice for a photograph, they felt a fifty-dollar bill. It was this small group that stood around in Mr. Morrow's kitchen about twilight on the day Janey turned seventeen.

It was as odd a gathering as you might imagine. I mean, this was another kind of girl, a girl above and distant from us, and this was her party. She moved quietly among the girls and boys while we all talked to Mr. Morrow in the kitchen as he set out paper cups and a bowl of punch and a small tray of crackers. He was glad we had come. He was happy to meet Janey's classmates. He worked at the Texaco refinery. On and on he talked. I realized that he wasn't used to talking, that this was all a kind of spillage brought on by the clear relief that anyone at all had come to Janey's party. This was fun, he said. A party. With the famous Evil Eye! He smiled. He was proud of Janey, her schoolwork; after all, she worked so hard, and being without a mom and all, and he was glad, well, to meet her classmates. We all nodded at him and finally the girls came and got the tray of crackers and poured everyone a cup of the red punch and it was enough to shake everybody up and have them go into the little living room, and when the girls had sat down in the chairs, and the boys had piled in on the floor, and Mr. Morrow had come into the doorway with his glass of punch, someone turned off all the lights but one, a desk lamp under which Janey Morrow must have been doing her trigonometry homework for the first eon of her life without knowing the next was about to begin. When all these things were accomplished, I came forward, looking worried, and unfolded our little table before the assemblage, shook out the tablecloth, and set out the Mysterious Objects.

That night, though the story has a thousand variations, there were only three. Evil Eye had worn the sunglasses to a football game the previous Friday and they were lost—another mystery, he told me, when I asked him where they were—and so I set out the pair of brass doorknobs, the metal bucket handle, and the pink plastic shoehorn. I'd learned by now to add a little drama to my part, so after they were set on the table, I went back to my station by the wall and then I returned to the table and I adjusted the doorknobs, the shoehorn, as if they needed to be just right for everything to work. Then I stepped back and gave them a dire look as if I could

see Fate itself. Evil Eye came from behind me, his robe drag-
ging the floor, and handed me our fat black candle, and I set
that on the exact center of the table and lit a kitchen match
and handed it to him and he looked at the yellow flame as if it
were a ragged peephole to the future, that is with a face as
serious and blank as he could make it, and he ceremoniously
lit the candle, reached back without looking, and handed me
the smoking matchstick.

I then pointed to the desk lamp and said my line: "Could
we have the flow of electric current to that device interrupted?" As always there was a pause, a "What'd he say?" and
finally someone reached up and turned off the light. The
light now collapsed to the point of the pulsing candle and
back along the still profile of Evil Eye Allen. Something was
moving behind his back, flying, flapping toward his face, and
it became his hand as it fell across his eyes. He stood there like
that, like a man in deep concentration or grief. In the new
dark he had our attention again.

Evil Eye turned his head toward the gathering. His hand,
as it had so often, stayed right where it had been in space, a
disconnected force, a separate thing suddenly joined by
another thing, a hand in the dark, and then his hands began
to float upward and I could see their movement mirrored by
every chin in the room. Heads lifted. Every eye followed the
hands to their apex and held there. I mean, this was fifteen
seconds and he had the entire room in the palms of his raised
hands. From where I stood, I could just see the candlelight on
the faces turned toward Evil Eye and the occasional sharp
glimmer off somebody's glasses. This view was cut into by the
dark form of Evil Eye himself, that gown, his raised arms,
and so I couldn't see everything he was doing. I knew that he
could draw his face into a tight vortex that looked unearthly,
bunching his eyebrows down and pulling his mouth up, and

then send the parts of his face to the far corners of the field, creating a look best described as being *inhabited*. I don't know if he was doing this or not.

But I did see his arms fall and the candle flutter, and then he pulled something from inside his robe and held it up, and this was a large red handkerchief. We could all see it. He knelt. He stood. He waved his arm slowly in a big arc, back and forth. Then he stopped. Everyone was watching that handkerchief, and we saw his hand begin to finger it into his palm, slowly gathering it the way a spider eats larger prey, and the look on the faces I could dimly see was a kind of fear. When it was consumed, his fist closed like a rock. It had a kind of pulse, a beat from where I stood, as if the cloth wanted out, and then I saw his hand tremble and falter and it began to open slowly.

I'm trying to be accurate.

The red handkerchief lifted like a little fire and stood on his open palm with a life of its own. For a moment it seemed the only light in the room.

Then the next part, the famous part, began with a scrape, a knee pop somewhere in the middle of the room, and a figure arose and this was Janey Morrow. Her eyes made two pools of wavering light on her face. This is the part that Evil Eye wanted me to be delicate with, the way the other kids parted to let her drift forward, a look on her face of confidence and ease and utter attention. She came up to Evil Eye and her posture changed in a moment and forever as she straightened up and lifted her face, and I could see her look into his eyes, and what was reflected was something private, and I regret the imprecision of that phrase, but I'm certain of it. The look was something private and I saw her eyes open even wider with it, and then she turned and took the handkerchief from where it stood on his hand. She said, "You're right. This is mine. Thank you."

Her voice was already different, clear and tender.

Evil Eye pointed to the table, the candle, the Mysterious Objects. Janey Morrow went to the table and picked up the doorknobs, hefting them into both hands. She turned back to Evil Eye with an expression of unparalleled joy. I'm a writer and careful of such phrases, but I'm using it now because it is the truth. I'm trying to leave nothing out.

He reached out with two fingers and touched the doorknobs and said in a whisper that everyone heard, "You are now free to do whatever you like."

That was it. I'd never heard him say such a thing before. He had said, "What is it you'd like to say?" and "Tell us the headlines," the responses being various and not without meaning: "My mother has fixed me breakfast all my life," "It takes years for the right rain to fall," things like that.

But then Evil Eye said, "You are now free to do whatever you like," and he stepped back so close to me that the hem of his garment was on my shoes, and Janey Morrow, who was already taller than she'd been a moment before, started to do a little dance, that is turn and step happily as she turned. Her face shone with what I'll call sureness, and she raised those doorknobs above her head. She was twirling like that, a movement which I'm sure was an expression of happiness, and the twirling was getting a little faster, her skirt in a flare, and we could hear her breath and see her white legs visible in the unreliable light. This was a person who did not dance in front of people, a girl who had never really behaved in such a way. She had never been among us. Now she stopped and her mouth was open and breathing and her eyes looked glad and she went to Evil Eye and handed him the doorknobs.

"Isn't this why we're here?" she said, turning back to the group. "Isn't this why we're here?" She lifted her black sweater up suddenly over her head, and there against her white skin was the red handkerchief like a bikini top, and then it billowed and fell. Her breasts lit the room like floating fires. The silence roared. I could see the teeth in Janey Morrow's gleeful smile. Then her sweater came down on my head and I stumbled against the table.

It was I who bumped the table. It was not Evil Eye or Janey Morrow. Though I'm not sure now it matters. Janey kicks the table in some versions, which is not true, and in some versions she heaves the table over, which is not true, and in some versions the candles catch the curtains and fire chases people from the room, which is not true, and the fire department comes, which they did not, and Janey and her father have to move to Bark City, and Evil Eye, almost consumed in the blaze, is disfigured and still moves among us, a driven ghost, inhabiting our dreams. That last part might be on target.

So now I'll just say it, what happened. I bumped the table and it shivered sharply and collapsed, spilling the remaining Mysterious Objects and our candle onto our front-row spectators. The flickering light in the room rocked, flared, and slid, and in the new dark we all could still see her breasts, bright ghosts in air.

Mr. Morrow turned the lights on, and the scene may as well have been turned inside out, light to shadow, shadow to light, a dozen blinking teenagers scrambling up in the blooming confusion. "Did you see that?" Benjamin Putnam said. "What was that?" But before he'd finished, two things happened that I witnessed close hand. Evil Eye, stock still and looking surprised for the first time I knew him, locked eyes with Janey Morrow. She had her sweater, that mystery, back on. Their look was as serious as looks get, and I could never read such things, but this one said something like: Something ends here, something begins.

What literally happened next is that Mr. Morrow crossed the room in two steps, pushed me aside and, lifting Evil Eye to his toes in the raw light, struck him in the face. It was this act that closed the party down. Suddenly there was a lot of scurrying, hauling one another up and out, and we were in the car.

I remember that drive well. Evil Eye was silent, driving the car with one hand over his eye. He turned to me a couple of times as if checking my face for some understanding: Did I see what just happened? Finally, after he'd driven me home, he said to me, "We'll have to get the table next week. Remember, Rick, we've got the Fergusons tomorrow. Four o'clock. Be there." I wanted to ask him what he'd seen in Janey's eyes. I wanted to ask him what about our candles and the Mysterious Objects. And somewhere inside of me I wanted to ask him if he'd planned the whole thing, if he'd been in control the entire time. There was something about him that day, something different, beyond the wacky act he'd been doing. I wanted to think it was power, but it might have been sadness.

We did the Fergusons, of course, and after that we were in utter demand and we raised our rates again and worked steadily. He'd appeared there with his left eye swollen shut, a purple thing that made your own eyes water to look at. To peek at it made your eyes water. Evil Eye indeed, Mr. Ferguson said. Everyone said. I wanted people to call me Igor, regardless of Mr. Trachtenberg's wrath, but no one did. The name appeared in our programs, but everyone just called me Rick. We worked all over the state. Before I left for college we had earned almost nine thousand dollars.

What happened to me that spring is only part mystery to me now. The week of graduation, Mr. Trachtenberg asked for his trig book back, and I thought certainly it was the termination of my hopes for passing, for graduating on time, and I thought I would be six weeks in summer school. He'd given me no clue as to my ranking, my mark, how I was doing. When I brought it in, he thanked me and set it on his desk beside something I'd seen before: a pair of brass doorknobs. Seeing them gave me a strange feeling that was confirmed on my report card: Trigonometry—A. It is now part of my permanent record, as is the look that Janey Morrow gave me when I returned to my seat. Her face had changed, or so I'll say, and I looked right at her and asked, "What did you do?"

She smiled and I could see it there in the second smile I'd ever seen on her face, a face I'd barely seen, a face new in the world and held high. "Mr. Trachtenberg must not believe you're the devil's assistant any longer," she said. Her confidence was overwhelming.

That spring I came to know that she and Evil Eye were quietly dating, though I never saw them together. Things swim under the surface of our lives and there are times when you can sense the rhythms and other times when you can't. Janey sat next to me in trig, and I might as well have been sitting by Evil Eye; all the vibrations came through. When he and I went to our shows, her presence was in the car. He had entered her perimeter. When student body elections came along, Janey ran for student body president. The list was published, and you could hear people in the hallways reading her name and saying, "Why is the snob doing that?" She had been apart from or above everything, and now here she was entering the fray.

Evil Eye and I went to the gym for the election assembly, where each of the kids running for office got to say a little something for two minutes. His eye was better, but he got a reception everywhere he went, signals from boys and girls, odd waves, recognition of his talents. It was almost as if, when we ascended the rows of bleachers, everyone acknowledged him because not to would be to invite harm. Some kids just tugged his shirttail or bumped his leg in passing; everybody touched the Evil Eye.

Onstage were twelve well-scrubbed students acting like

little senators or comedians and sometimes both, telling a joke and then saying, "But seriously, we citizens of Orkney High . . ." When they called Janey's name, she stood and came forward on the polished hardwood floor. She was wearing a slim maroon business suit, the skirt a lesson in rectitude, the shoulders of her short jacket flared in a lift that framed her face in a heartbreaking curve. Her speech was one sentence: "I'm asking you to remember that we're all human." Then she bowed her head slightly and pulled a red handkerchief from her bodice and waved it twice. Janey walked back to her seat in the loudest ovation ever created in that fine and ancient edifice. I looked at Evil Eye, his grin, the tears rimming his eyes.

It was the first assembly we'd ever attended, and it would also be the last. Our custom was to spend assembly time alone in the middle of the football bleachers. Evil Eye would stretch out over three or four seats and set his hand out as if to hold the gymnasium and all of its occupants, and he would say, "Did I tell you about growing up in Orkney, about going to high school in America?"

"You did," I'd always say. "We're still here."

His face would roll to mine and he'd smile as if at a child and say, "My dear Rick, that would be the wrong answer." And then he'd begin what I see now was a kind of rambling poem about being seventeen, a word he said was a central part of the code of the unknown, and he would invert himself so his head was far below and his magnificent feet were in my face, and he would go on and offer me all the advice I would need if I was going to be a writer.

AT COPPER VIEW

ON A WARM, BLOND OCTOBER afternoon years ago, Daniel Hamblin jogged around the cinder track of his high school. His football practice uniform was stained with dirt and grass and soaked with sweat, and the heavy costume felt nothing but good on his young body as he worked through his third of four after-practice laps. He was a boy with words for things, and in the rhythm of his run, he thought, I'm seventeen and I'm in love. Many things will happen this year to me for the first time. When he spoke this way, his buddy Qualls would say, "Right, boss." Around the oval track his teammates were strung at intervals, their cleats crunching the fine red cinders as they ran. All the forty red helmets were scattered in the end zone where these young men had tossed them, as was their custom before last laps. Daniel Hamblin loved this, the long shadows of the gymnasium falling across the track, the strength he felt in his lungs and legs, his sense of everything happening as he commented on it. "You old building," he said aloud.

It was always four laps, no stopping, and Daniel Hamblin ran four laps, always finishing among the first few players, picking up his helmet and going into the gym. There was a group of boys on the team who were always last, who shuffled so slowly around the track that they were inevitably lapped and lost to the sequence of things, purposefully really, and they picked up their helmets after three laps, joining the file into the gym. One of these boys was the center of the football team, a wry and popular guy named Deke Overby, who was also co-captain. He was a roughneck with a good head of red hair and a face of freckles that looked manly on him, and he was admired, as certain athletes are in the fall of the year, for strength and confidence and his wide-open sense of humor. As the boys stripped off their soaked uniforms and hung their pads on the drying hangers and peeled off their jockstraps, Deke Overby kind of ran the room, calling questions to the various players about what they had done just now during practice or what was the deal with some girl they were seeing, and these were good things, not unwholesome, and it made the guys smile as they stood soaping in the steamy shower, and each boy was hoping Deke would pick him out and say, "If you tackle that hard in practice, two things are going to happen: you're going to hurt old Qualls here, and we're going to kick butt on Saturday at Highland," or some such.

Daniel Hamblin loved the locker room. He liked having his gear stowed and he favored pulling on his oxford cloth school shirts and standing there on his discarded towel in his boxer shorts, his thick black hair in wet disarray, buttoning the shirt. It would be dark by the time they departed the gymnasium, and he loved riding home with his longtime neighbor Qualls, who also played defensive end and who was quiet and tough. They rode home with the windows down even as the nights had cooled, watching the lighted storefronts of their town pass by, not talking.

Daniel felt a new waking, a special distance from his life that made him feel part of a story, a character. It all felt like an amazing backdrop. "We're teenage boys involved in American high-school football, driving home from practice." Qualls would shake his head and say, "Right, boss."

Tonight as Daniel Hamblin pushed open the heavy gym

doors and felt the October air come at his neck, he heard his name. It was Deke Overby, one sleeve in his letter jacket, hustling up the locker-room steps. "Dan," Overby said. "Listen, do you think you could do me a favor?" Daniel waved at Qualls across the street opening the doors of his Pontiac; he'd be right there. He was a little stunned that Deke Overby even knew his name, and now they were talking. "My girlfriend goes to Copper View. Do you know Holly?"

"I don't think so," Daniel said. Everyone knew Deke had a very steady girl who went somewhere else to school. Copper View was out beneath the copper mine, clear across the valley.

"Holly's girlfriend Jackie is queen of their homecoming this Saturday and she doesn't have a date." Deke had squared his jacket and now zipped the front and thrust his hands into the pockets. "You're a nice guy. We gotta do the right thing. Think we could double? As a favor? I'll drive."

Daniel smiled; he wasn't sure what was being asked. "Sure," Daniel said "Sounds good."

"Great," Overby said. "It is. She's the queen of the damn thing." He tapped Daniel's head. "So be sure to comb your hair. We'll be the only two Cougars there."

Daniel Hamblin's friend Laura Sumner understood the arrangement. "It's a favor," she told him. "You're good to do it." They were sitting on the side steps of the old main building in the weak fall sun, having their lunch. Laura's mother made tomato sandwiches on homemade wheat bread, and she traded these for his own bologna and mustard white-bread creations. When she unwrapped them, she had to peel them apart and realign the bread. "A homecoming queen cannot go unattended."

"I guess," Daniel said. They had been meeting for lunch for three weeks, exchanging notes for two, and they had kissed on these old stone steps one week ago and every day since.

And. There had been a tussle. Three days before at Laura's house in front of the television, half on the rug and half on the couch, they'd had a moment. They had been to the school play, which had been *Gidget*, a bright thing to behold, full of their classmates with thick makeup tans. Laura was reviewing the play for the school paper and she'd asked Daniel along. After a bottle of 7Up and twenty minutes of *The Late Show*, their embrace closed out the world, and they slid down, gracefully and awkwardly, until at one juncture when they had to shift, Laura said, "We're acting a lot like we're about to have sex." This took a moment to register in Daniel, and when it did he was hurt, and started to apologize. She put her hand on his mouth. "Stop," she whispered. "We are." Her eyes were bright. "I hope." She kissed him. "But not here. My parents are right down there." She pointed to the hall. "Getting caught would spoil it for me." Her smile against his face caused him to smile, and they sat like that for a long moment, not exactly laughing, but close to it, happy to have this dear understanding between them.

Now on the old school steps, Daniel asked, "Is it going to make me something? Besides her date, I mean."

"Like king?" Laura Sumner said. "You can't step in at the last minute as a blind date and be king. There'll be a king, but he'll have been elected, too, and with his own date."

Daniel fished in his lunch sack for the Baggie of crushed potato chips, offering it to Laura. "They elect the king. It should be president or chairman."

"Czar," she said.

They sat on the old side steps because they could be alone and look across the street at the little Favorite Pharmacy, a throwback edifice, its windows plastered with specials and discounts years old. Most days they talked about the people coming and going, what they were after and why, and when a person came out with the little white Favorite bag, Laura or Daniel would comment about how much better everything was going to be for that person very soon. "He's warts from neck to toe," Daniel said about a man all in khaki. "He's all bumps, can't sleep. Contracted a wicked case of wartarama in the jungles of Arkansas."

"He's talking to the pharmacist right now," Laura picked it up. "Saying he's got a friend that is worried he might have a touch of wartsomething, like . . . a . . . wartarama!"

"Don't give me that," Daniel said in the voice of the pharmacist. "You don't have a friend now and you never will until you get rid of those warts. I can see them poking out of your clothing."

"You need this!" Laura mocked a commercial and held up her little lunch sack. "Wart-All-Gone! One treatment and you'll be smooth as a baby's bottom."

"And then maybe I could get some sleep," Daniel said.

"Oh, you'll need something else for sleep."

When the man came out a moment later, they laughed because he was carrying a huge cardboard box of something they could not read. "That man is taking the big cure!" Laura said. "He feels better already!" Laughing, their heads fell together in a way that Daniel Hamblin loved, and their faces were close when they turned and looked at each other, and with their eyes open, they kissed. Then they closed their eyes and they kissed again. They stayed close and he could smell the dry, clean scent off her face. He loved that it was so clear that they were both willing to kiss again. Finally, Laura sat up and took a few of the crumbly potato chips.

"At the dance, what should I call her?" he said. "Your majesty?"

"What's her name?" Laura said. "This girl, your queen?"

"Overby said her name is Jackie."

Laura Sumner, who usually was very funny about Daniel's hurriedly made sandwiches, stopped eating then and began to put her lunch away. Daniel watched her and said simply, "I'll call her Jackie."

It was a strange week for Daniel, the first strange week in his life really, because he realized that the feelings that pulled him this way and that were his feelings now, his responsibility, and this thought, which he had on Monday as he sat on the old steps on the side of the high school and Laura Sumner did not show up, made him feel terrified and powerful. Deke Overby buddied up to him at practice, pulling him into the first circle of guys there, hauling at his shoulder pads and talking to him as if they were old friends, good friends, and this made him feel elevated and unreal; he liked it. He'd come into the coach's view somehow and his name was called more frequently. Laura Sumner did not show up Tuesday either, and he ate his stupid sandwiches and crushed chips alone, watching the people file in and out of Favorite Pharmacy. He pointed at each as they emerged and said quietly, "You're cured. You're cured." He missed Laura, a feeling primarily in his stomach, a hurt. She was in his Biology II class right before lunch, and the fact that he saw her there, knew where she was every minute, and then that she didn't join him on the steps, made him sorry and proud. The cool north shadow of the big building was a lonely place now.

He rode home from practice every night with Qualls and they stopped at the Blue Bird and ate the forty-nine-cent cheeseburgers, three or four of them with the vanilla shake, fries, and icy Cokes, sitting on the old wooden picnic tables under the Blue Bird's buzzing fluorescent lights. Qualls had a system: he unwrapped his burgers, unfolding the yellow paper and peeling the top bun off to remove the four pickle slices and stacking them on the paper. He didn't like the pickles. The boys ate and watched Qualls's pickles stack up. Daniel's hair dried. When they talked, they talked with their mouths full, and if Qualls was through removing the pickles from his sandwich, he gestured with it when he spoke.

"So, you going with your buddy Overby this weekend?"

"I'm escorting the queen of Copper View's homecoming."

"That's where his wife goes."

"That's what he said," Daniel replied. "Why does everybody say that?"

"That's what he calls her. They're way into it. He stays out there some weekends. There's a ring. He hasn't told you this stuff? I thought you'd know the color of her underpants by now, you guys are such good buddies."

"Come on, Jeff. I'm just doing him a favor."

Qualls balled the yellow burger paper tightly in his fist. "Well," he said, standing up now and stepping out of the picnic table, "it hasn't hurt you in practice."

"Jeff . . ."

"Hey." Qualls plucked his paper shake cup from the table and drew on the straw. "If you start against Fairmont Friday night, you and Overby will be way even."

On Saturday, Deke Overby picked Daniel up at six and they drove across the valley toward Copper View. Deke was driving his father's Oldsmobile, a huge car featuring plenty of chrome; he'd washed it up and the heavy car shined in the new evening. Deke smelled of aftershave. His hair was combed over severely and his sport coat was folded over the front seat-back. The radio was playing on KNAK, the cool station. Daniel liked this and he could feel the world pulling at him.

It was a pleasure, the world calling him, and he listened to it. He had started in the game yesterday against Fairmont, and Qualls had played second platoon end. He'd done well,

stepping into the expanded role with a toughness that surprised him at first. Every time the Fairmont line would roll
his way, he'd fend them off one by one, delaying the sweep
long enough for the linebackers to come up and crush the
play. It was more contact than he'd ever had in an afternoon,
and late in the day at the end of the third quarter, when the
shadow of the Fairmont Science Building fell across the south
end of the Fairmont football field, which was lush and torn
up, Daniel felt a happiness fill his body, his shoulders and his
hips, his wrists and his knees, that was beyond thinking,
beyond his words for it. He could not have identified or
expressed it, but it came off him in waves. At first he had
wondered if Laura Sumner had made the drive, was at the
game, and then thoughts of her—and everything else—
dropped away and he was taken by the work before him. He
had been waiting to find out what running and diving and
rolling and getting back up were all about, and now he just
committed them all again and again. When the game ended
there was still more in him; he could have played and played.
Everyone knew he had made a mark and would start the rest
of the season.

This had all happened in a week, this step, whatever it was
that had him now in his new gray tweed sport coat with Deke
Overby headed out of town. Laura Sumner had come by their
stone steps finally on Friday at the end of lunch. He'd sat
there every day savoring something bittersweet he had no
name for, something real, though, a little loss. She stood above
him in a blue and gray kilt, the gold pin in it maddeningly
beyond his comprehension. There was a matching gold pin
on the heart of her gray sweater.

"Hello," he said. When she didn't answer, he said, "I
already ate all the chips. Sit down?"

Laura sat down and hugged her knees. They watched the
front of Favorite Pharmacy until two women came out clos-

ing their purses and talking. The two women got in a white Ford pickup and drove away. Daniel looked into Laura's face, her eyes, and the hot glance held until her eyes teared. They heard the bell ring deep in the building, but neither Daniel nor Laura moved. After a while the second bell rang. "Now we're late," Daniel said.

"You're late," she told him. "I'm going to give it all a rest." She stood and walked down the stairs toward the parking lot in the rear.

"I'm doing it as a favor to Overby," Daniel said to her. "You know that and I know that."

She stopped below him and once again folded her arms. "Well," she said up to him before leaving him there. "That's everybody."

He knew from the feeling that then rose in him, the space that opened, that he was in love with Laura Sumner, and it wasn't all a good feeling, some of it made him feel older than he ever wanted to be. For the first time in his life, he put his forehead in his hand and closed his eyes and sat still.

Copper View was a rough little town of small houses on dirt lanes. Everything needed painting and nothing would be painted, because the copper mine was slowly and inevitably moving down the mountain. The IGA grocery was boarded up and the little string of shops on Main Street looked sad. In the early evening, the place had the look of an ancient village, the green weeds growing to the street, the hedges unruly, and the huge poplars and cottonwoods just beginning to change. Deke Overby pulled the big Olds onto the gravel margin in front of a tiny house overgrown with roses and sego lilies. Holly appeared and at first Daniel thought she was somebody's little sister, a short blond girl in a strapless blue satin dress. Then she pulled Deke into a serious kiss, practiced and resolute, there on the walkway, the two of them folding together urgently. Daniel, three steps away, didn't dare approach. Finally, Deke put Holly down, and she looked at Daniel and said, "Oh, Jackie can't wait to meet you. This is going to be such fun. You are such an angel. Come on in!"

The house was in fact very small and dark. In the little living room a woman watched television and did not move as they passed through. In the small kitchen a young woman stood, arms folded, against the counter in a shiny red dress. Daniel looked at her in surprise. He hadn't prepared in any way for meeting this person, and stumbling through the narrow space had dislocated him enough that he quickly double-checked to see if anyone else, his real date, was in the room. "Jackie!" Holly said. "This is Daniel." His custom was to nod as he shook hands, and he did this, taking Jackie's lotioned hand in his and nodding. From that touch, he was unmoored. This person was something else. All girls were older than you were; he was used to that. But having never seen her in street clothes, coming across her in this ridiculous kitchen with its little windows run with vines, and beside her dark curly hair, a gold clock in a red rooster, and her red dress held to her somehow by the blue shadow between her breasts, a shadow he would not look at, though he knew by the hard glow coming off the top of each side of it where it was at all times, Daniel had no chance to regroup, to consider Jackie a friend or even a person his own age going to a school dance.

The rest of the night was like that: a vertiginous drift. They got in the Oldsmobile and went up the hill to the old high school, a building in the Georgian style, built a hundred years before. Jackie took Daniel's hand on the way up the steps to the gymnasium, seized it tightly, oddly, and she would not let it go. The ceiling of the small gym was an undulating landscape of streamers, hanging like thick moss, and a five-person combo played slow jazz from one corner. Lights blinked in the waving dark, and Daniel couldn't figure out the motif. It was as if they were underwater.

Deke and Holly moved off immediately and locked into their embrace, which because she was so short against him looked only sexual, which Daniel could see it was. In the first hour a dozen couples came by and hugged Jackie, and the girls chatted happily with her, issuing little squeals about her dress, while the boys stood back in their sport coats and looked at Daniel. None of them spoke to him, although he greeted them all. He remembered Deke's words about being Cougars at the Miners' homecoming. Jackie held his hand the entire time.

The coronation ceremony, too, unsettled him. The music stopped and someone, a man who might have been a coun selor or a history professor, spoke into a microphone from a small platform at one end of the gym. He said some names. Then the music started again, a kind of ceremonial pomp, and a spotlight that only blinded the room shot from behind the man, creating a kind of hot corridor, and into this corridor first one couple walked toward the light and then another couple. These were the runner-ups. Their shadows crashed through the room crazily. Daniel heard Jackie's name and then his name as "escort," and suddenly they were out on the floor, now arm in arm, walking toward the light. He could see the little white faces outside the spotlight watching him, and even in the glare and through the music, he could hear them asking who he was, who is that with Jackie, who is that guy. He helped crown Jackie and someone handed her a rose that she waved. Then the king came up with his date, another girl with bare shoulders, and he was crowned and waved his fist to all the applause.

The king and queen danced the next dance. Daniel stepped off the back of the short platform in the dark and for the first time tonight he was alone, and he thought of Laura Sumner, what she would make of any of this. He wanted to tell her about it, so she could see his role. It seemed stupid and wrong to have lost any part of his friendship with her over all this. He was doing Deke Overby a favor and it was everything but over now. He'd walked in the searchlight under the scary streamers.

Now he felt a tap at his shoulder and there were two guys there, big guys, one in a maroon blazer and one in a dark Sunday suit. "Who are you?" the boy in the suit said.

"Daniel Hamblin. I'm a friend of Deke Overby's."

"Who?"

"Holly's squeeze," the maroon blazer told his friend.

"What are you doing with Jackie?" The boy in the suit was upset about something.

"I'm her date," Daniel said. Something had made him decide not to give these two any help. "We're at the home-coming."

"You're out of place," the suit said. "You have crossed the line." He came forward into Daniel's face. "You make me sick."

The three boys were very close now behind the platform, but Daniel could tell there wouldn't be a fight. He understood that and considered offering a smart rejoinder and then passed on that, too. What the hell. This was all too weird. He would save it, the blazer, the sick line, the whole story, for Laura. There was something about knowing this would all be part of a story that made him happy and very confident. He had a distance and a safety they knew nothing about. They were in his story and he'd tell it on the old stone steps.

The music had been over for a while, and here came Jackie now, her tiara in her rich hair. "Hello, Blaine," she said to the boy in the suit as if she knew how they'd been talking.

"Hello, Bobby." She took Daniel's hand again. "Daniel, shall we dance?"

The next hour was the deciding hour. As soon as Daniel took her in his arms, the evening changed. She filled his arms and moved very close against him. He knew how to dance, had known the seven things there are to know about dancing, but this was changing those notions. First, in the first minute, she took her right hand from his left and laid it along his neck, and after looking into his face for five and then ten seconds, she brought her head up and fitted it against the side of his face. Their modified waltz collapsed into a slow two-step, which left him drifting against her legs, the muscles there, under the waving ceiling. He could also feel her hands clenched in the back of his coat, and her arms up over his shoulders, and the swelling front of her as it worked against his chest with their every small motion. Lost in this, he pulled her closer, too, his hands on the small of her back, but when he did, she started suddenly and pushed away. She looked alarmed and held him at arm's length, still dancing. Okay, he thought, okay, and he felt the saving distance come back.

"What are you doing here?" she whispered to him.

"Jackie," he said, "I'm only . . ."

Her head again rose to his shoulder and nestled there and her hands ran around his neck, tighter this time, her body, each contour now finding him, sending him. His eyes closed immediately, but then he opened them by will, scanning the crowd for watching faces as he felt Jackie's body in conspiracy with his own in the old gymnasium of Copper View High School.

His distance was gone in a moment and long gone. He was careful not to pull her or press his luck. Regardless, two or three minutes into their descent, Jackie again pushed away, her eyes wide, moving away from him entirely, and he had begun to feel the cool air against his neck where her hand had been, when she took his hand and pulled him steadily through the room and out the double doors. He didn't ask, just followed her down the stairs a flight and out the back school doors into the small faculty parking lot, where the sandy yellow tailings spilled in a steep fan onto the asphalt. In two years the school would be parted out, the bricks sold to a gardening nursery in Salt Lake City, the doors to contractors, and the wooden gym floor itself to a company that used it all in two summer homes for movie stars fifty miles south above Provo Canyon. The price of copper would go up twelve cents a ton, and the mine would step down the mountain a half mile a year until every step, vine, and trellis in the village was buried.

Now, beginning to feel the grit under his dress shoes, Daniel was stopped by this young woman in her red dress. Her tiara, remarkably, was still straight. It was dark here even with the lamp above the back door of the school, and they could only see the edge of things. But he could see her face. She had a strange look on her face, which Daniel thought was probably a good sign, given the elevated state they were in. Her eyes were on his.

"Hey, mister," she said and pushed him back onto the side of someone's Ford.

"Hey," he said.

Now she kissed him and kissed him again, taking the kisses like something both stolen and expected, her hands on the sides of his head and then behind his neck and up into his hair and then back on his face. He knew now, as he suspected in the gym, that he had given over any control of the night. Between kisses, their bodies close, she whispered, "Okay, mister," and "Hey, mister," and "This here, mister." When he opened his eyes he saw the insane alluvial fan behind them looking like a stopped landslide, a geologic reprieve.

It became overtly physical. Jackie hitched up her dress a bit and stood him against the car with authority, and now she was kissing him and tugging at his hair, and pressing against him, and now she ran her hands down the front of him, grabbing at him and whispering through what seemed to him smiling teeth, "Okay, mister, mister."

The little pullings of his hair and some of her bumpings were tough and her hands where no one's hands, except his, had ever been wanted to wake Daniel, but he was paralyzed. Whatever was going to happen was going to happen.

"Jackie!"

Even after her name was called again, Jackie didn't relent with Daniel. Then she was being removed from him. It was, of course, the boy in the Sunday suit.

"God damn you," he said, and he stepped up almost to where Jackie had been seconds before. Now Daniel knew there would be a fight, and his mind was reeling sentences again, one being: Of course there was a fight. That's what that little faculty lot was used for on weekends. He loved his stupid logic, even though he was frightened.

"Hit him, Blaine!" Daniel turned to see the maroon blazer step in front of Jackie, her tiara still straight, and he turned again so that the fight could begin, so that Bobby could hit him in the side of the face, which he did. It hurt, which was awful for Daniel, but there it was again, the distance coming back, the logic; he hit me and it hurt. Life makes sense. Then Bobby lifted a knee sharply into Daniel and the logic, too, was gone.

They wrestled for a while and Daniel actually fought back some, though he knew his role was to lose this fight in such a way that Bobby could have his story, too. Daniel was mad at moments, lost, too, in the anger, but never far below the surface. He hit the kid a couple of times, pushed his face, grabbed him, a tackle, and they both rolled and sat in the soft dirt slope, filling their shoes and pockets with the sour golden sand spilling down from the open-pit copper mine.

Such fights end when there's blood and when one of the members refuses to get up, and both conditions had been met within five minutes. Five minutes is a long time. Five minutes allows the person with the right emotional distance to compose and revise the entire story, make a crucial decision about the sexual parts of such a story and then adjust that decision and find and phrase the exact words for the event. After five minutes of fighting with Bobby, Daniel had been beaten. He knew he'd been beaten early, and then was certain when his face hit the asphalt and the skin on his cheekbone burned. He sat up in the sandy corner of the parking lot and shook his head. Five minutes before, he'd been in an embrace with Jackie, and now everyone was gone, and he listened to the grains of sand whisper down the slope and fill the cavities around his hands.

He stood by Deke's car on a side street down from the school to empty sand from his clothing. He shook his jacket and threw it on the hood. He removed his shoes and struck them against each other, and part by part, moving carefully in chilly fall air, he shook out all his clothes and put them back on.

The first time Laura Sumner had passed him a folded note, it was as they were leaving biology, and he thought of that moment now as the first moment in all of this. It was a sheet of notebook paper folded up the size of a playing card. He felt it as something powerful, and he wandered heedless past his locker and his buddies, ending on the side steps of the school, where he sat down and unfolded the paper with care. It was early in the school year and his life was opening. He loved being alone with that note. It was a high, sharp feeling that he tried to keep. A week later they started telling stories about the customers of Favorite Pharmacy.

Now his face hurt vaguely and he could still feel sand inside his shirt. He sat on the curb and thought of himself outside of everything. He was sitting on the curb when Deke and Holly came up.

"Where you been, Danny?" Deke Overby said.

"We looked all around for you and Jackie," Holly added. Her hair was all crooked now, mashed on the side she kept against Deke's rib cage while they danced. Daniel told them the story, an abbreviated version, to which Holly said, "Oh, yeah, that makes sense. She'd go home with Bobby."

"Is Bobby her boyfriend?" Daniel asked.

"Oh God, no," Holly said. "God, no."

There were two more episodes after the homecoming, but only one would work its way in Daniel Hamblin's story. The three of them, Daniel in the big backseat, drove the ten blocks to Holly's house, where there was a light on, and when they arrived, Holly said, "Mom's still up."

"No problem," Deke said. He made a kind of knowing nod back at Daniel, which Daniel, having never seen such a thing, did not know how to interpret. Deke nudged Holly and her head disappeared into his lap, and Daniel leaned back in his seat. When Daniel realized what he was listening to, he opened his door, saying sorry when the dome light went on, and he walked slowly down the block. He walked in the center of the quiet street and he could feel and hear sand all about him. He walked until he came to an open yard where he could see a dog sleeping on an unfinished porch, and he turned and started back. Then he stopped, and feeling his beating pulse in his abraded cheek, Daniel just looked up.

Deke Overby would graduate high school with Daniel and opt to go on his mission for his church that fall. He'd get assigned to Tallahassee, and go out there with his missionary partner, a kid who was a year older who had graduated from Lincoln High. Deke Overby and Holly would get reported six months into it. She would have moved to Florida and set up a little apartment where he would visit her between conversions. It upset the kid from Lincoln. Such an arrangement runs counter to church policy and doctrine, and Deke would get excommunicated and return home and marry Holly.

When Daniel finally heard Deke honk and he walked back and climbed in the front seat of the big car, Deke winked at him and said, "Good thinking. I appreciate the privacy."

They started back with the windows down, but rolled them up when they hit the highway. It was cold. Deke was trying to tune in KNAK from out of town.

"What's the deal on Jackie?" Daniel asked.

"Nice girl. You're a good man to help out."

"What's her deal, Deke?" Sitting, Daniel could feel the sand he'd missed. "Is she crazy?"

Deke drove awhile. The radio wavered and finally settled. "Look," he said. "I probably should have told you. Old Jackie had a man, longtime boyfriend. From junior high. His name was David Dillon. Longtime. And he got killed last weekend, whatever, shot on the deer hunt. A terrible thing. You read about it?"

Daniel had heard about a boy accidentally killed in the Stansburys. It happened every deer season somewhere in Utah.

He looked at Deke Overby. There was nothing to say. He didn't want to know when they'd buried the boy, because he knew it would have been two or three days ago. He didn't want to ask anything. He had his distance now all right. He had wanted to choose it and not have it forced on him. The story of the night was all gone for him now. He had been so sure of it. He wanted like all young men to be out of the water when he told of his drowning, but that, he saw now, would never be the way.

Single Woman for
Long Walks on the Beach

Looking for a young woman for the chance to exchange intro-
ductory remarks and help on homework, particularly math
and social studies, perhaps the term project, the triptych display about continental drift, share pencils, markers, erasers
(including all those in the shapes of animals), and lunch, with
the possibility of swapping the store-bought Aunt Dorothy's
Bigrolls for homemade tomato sandwiches stuffed with slices
of sharp Cheddar, merging our potato chips on a paper plate,
talking about our childhood until the bell rings, keeping this
up—lunching—both in the cafeteria and on the front steps of
the school, until laughing one day, we decide to skip quickly
away in my car, a lark, that's what we'd share is this lark, driving the strange daytime streets while all our classmates suffer
under the confused rule of Mrs. Delmanrico and her versions
of what happened when the great land masses first pulled
apart, finally ending up at the Blue Bird Drive-In, empty in
the late afternoon, and sharing two malts, the strawberry and
the vanilla, the feeling encircling us certainly something, but
not something easily identifiable or given a name, just something new, and in that place, deciding to try for the senior
prom, laughing at it in fun—what a goofy, schoolboy thing to
do—but also laughing from that feeling and, well, joy, and in
two weeks after another set of lunches, sharing the senior
prom, including me picking you up in my freshly washed Bel

Air, and meeting your mother and your sister, your sister really giving me the once-over, and you in a dress, which is actually pink, believably pink, a pink that rescues that color once and for all, and then dancing at the prom, our first touch really, carefully committed in the old gymnasium, visiting with your friends and some of my friends, and dancing and sharing then the long walk to the car, but knowing as we felt the night air fall on our warm faces as we left the building that everything had changed now and the feeling we had at the Blue Bird Drive-In has now become a real thing we still don't have a name for, but we are forever different in the car, talking now about college, not kissing, afraid to really, talking about the future and pledging to write to each other when we go away to college, which we will do, daily, handwritten letters, full of the heartbreaking news of classes, social life, every mention of another person, male or female, engendering faint but genuine pangs of what we will only be able to call jealousy and longing, all sent by post over a period long enough for the price of a stamp to go up three cents and then meeting again at a graduation-summer geology seminar at the first morning's coffee and seeing everything by now quite clearly as the entire conference, all of geology, the very world disappears and we go as we never have gone to bed together that noon without words although they will come along, among them some we will be happy to pronounce, I do, as we're wed, two young people fresh and strong and ready for the next thing though it will be no single one thing now but five libraries, two extensive research projects, a baby and then another, four apartments and a house and then another house and a position, yes, geology, with some solar research, this being for an energy firm in a large Midwestern city and a basketball hoop on the front of the garage along with a free-throw line in chalk and growing children, a girl and a boy, who will annoy the neighbors into knowing their names, and

SINGLE WOMAN FOR LONG WALKS

there will be success, not small success, in the careers some
original work recognized and material well-being some weekend afternoons with the sound of a basketball on the driveway we'll eat sandwiches in the kitchen and with the desire
alive in the room it will be as if one time were all time and we
were back on the lawn at a school where we met and then
with the kids gone we'll clean the garage, the stuff we're stor-
ing, all the photos and schoolwork, and we will share the
lovely sound of the broom on that cement floor but time will
turn for me that's part of this deal, seventy-five percent of all
women outlive their husbands, and there'll be an era of you
sitting at my bedside as a simple fact this is later but still too
soon by my measure and the days will wash away, your hand
on my arm some and some days just the yellow light on the
wall. This is when I'll ask to walk on the beach and expect
you to talk to me, to walk me out in story along a beach, let's
make it on an island, far from the grinding continents, you
pick it, Kailua, Sans Souci, Waimanelo or further shorelines
and fill in the details please the texture of the sand, hardpack
or plush, and I'll want the surf what there is timid or crazed
and the smell of course and the walk itself, which direction
and how far with me on the ocean side most of the time as we
swing our arms and talk the way we've always talked, the
sweet real pleasure of reason and speculation, and whether
we're barefoot or not, my cuffs wet, we'll walk on the beach,
that's what we signed up for and when it grows dark we can
stroll back all the way and we can dine by candlelight, there
are never enough candles in a life, so there it is: late in the day
a walk on the beach and this tray of hospital lasagna in the
candlelight.

III

THE POTATO GUN

COOPER WAS IN THE GARAGE arguing with his son Trevor when the phone rang. He'd come out with a paper bag of recycling scraps, because he'd been cleaning his office all morning instead of finishing the last draft of his light-rail proposal. It was due. Cooper was fifty and he'd been forever like he was fifteen, putting things off while he groomed the dog or washed the car. His mother had always called him Last Minute Charley, and smiled at his success. Here he was writing a mass-transit report, which took as its theme: Get My Mother to Town! The board had loved his story about driving her every Thursday to the Metropolitan Scrabble Club.

Behind him now, his home office was spotless, mint, like new, and it felt like a dank, spider-choked hellhole. He was in hard procrastination mode. He could write, but he always did it at the last minute. He had been hoping to clean the garage next, one of his favorite places, but there was his boy Trevor with a friend, some small kid whose eyebrows met over his nose, and they had tools spread on the workbench and the floor, and were working on a long section of plastic pipe.

"What's the project?" Cooper had asked, hoping for a way in. He'd done a lot of stuff out here in fifteen years: hogans from Popsicle sticks, models of the atom from Styrofoam, a protein cell from a rubber pillow pad. The two fifteen-year-olds turned to him. Trevor was inserting a brass fitting into the pipe. "Looks cool."

Trevor said something.

"What is it?"

"Potato gun," the other boy said.

Cooper put his bag down and went over. Trevor had duct-taped a plastic liter soda bottle to the end of the four-foot pipe.

"This is Justin," Trevor said without looking up.

"It'll put a potato through a wall," Justin said.

Trevor gave his friend a look. "No it won't."

"Right through," Justin said, an expert. He reached and tried to wiggle the piece of brass. It was solid.

Cooper was trying to select from the things to say, because this is where he'd got it wrong forty times before. His son was the most interesting person Cooper had ever had to deal with, and he wasn't sure he could measure up. "Is this the Justin we're driving to the prom?"

"Yes, sir," the boy replied. "Are you taking your old car?" He pointed at the covered 1956 Chevrolet, which was Cooper's treasure.

"Yes we are." The boys were sophomores but had been asked to the junior prom by two junior girls. Justin hefted the pipe gun from Trevor's hands and asked, "Shall we test it?"

Cooper took the thing and spoke: "No, we won't be testing it today. Justin, check with us tomorrow, will you?"

"Sounds good. I'll call you later, Trev." Justin dropped and put on one Rollerblade, and set off that way: one shoe, one skate.

"We could have tested it, Dad."

Cooper didn't know how to hold the thing; it felt terrible. Trevor stepped up and pointed to the parts: "The butane chamber, the igniting hole, the barrel." He showed his father another piece of the white plastic pipe with a knob of tape on the end. "This is the ramrod."

"A potato gun," Cooper said. He could restrain himself no longer. "Whose idea is this? We can't shoot this."

"Justin's got one. They're totally safe."

Cooper found fatherhood a roller coaster. You were up on top, but not for long, and the whole thing felt a lot like you'd repaired it yourself. At night and in a hurry. His son was grown and had been taller than Cooper for two months. He wished it was a hogan, a huge hogan made of anything. He wished it was not a potato gun.

Trevor stood before him now, his shoulders a kind of accusation: *Things were going just fine here before you came around.* It reminded Cooper of an argument they'd had five or six years before when Trevor had ordered free plans for a helicopter out of the back of *Popular Science.* He had done so because the ad said: *You Need No License!* Cooper had been at his desk at the last minute on some project for the city, and he'd pushed his chair back. He didn't want his son in a helicopter. He actually said as much, "You're not flying a helicopter." He had said it loud so that Libby had come in and asked what was the matter. It was another moment when he was snagged on something and pulled from his footing; there was no way to explain his position. Trevor rolled his eyes and turned in disgust, this ten-year-old pilot. When the plans came, he taped them to his bedroom door for all the world to see. They were still there.

"What are you going to do with it?" Trevor asked.

"Just hold it until we find out."

"Find out what?" Trevor was putting the tools away on the pegboard: the hacksaw, the awl, the pliers. "You don't need to find anything out." He twisted the words back sarcastically. "Justin's got one; it's fine with his dad."

"I'm not going by what Justin or his dad say." He'd already formed a picture of that savage group blowing round holes in the block walls and the stucco houses. "I don't know," Cooper said, "if it's legal." He looked out the open garage door at the fresh spring day, now gone for him. "We may not be allowed to have this in the city." He hated how that sounded, but he was scared of the thing blowing up or hurting someone. Cooper's father would have said, "Let's go out and see what this baby can do," but it had skipped Cooper, that confidence.

Now in the garage, Trevor didn't respond. He had the tools up, and he swept the white plastic crumbs with a whisk broom. After a moment he turned and folded his arms and leaned back against the old workbench that Cooper had made the year the boy was born. Trevor looked at him, a full accusation: *You've ruined something again.*

"I just need to find out," Cooper said.

Trevor looked at his father and shook his head: wrong, wrong, wrong. "How are you going to find out?"

The potato gun was heavy in Cooper's arms. "I guess I'll just call over to the police and ask them." A Suburban drove slowly down the street and the Welchs looked in the garage at Cooper and the weapon.

"You're going to call the police?"

"I guess. Unless you've got a better idea. We just need some information." The last was Cooper's fallback. His own folks had always said, "We'll see," and it had always been maddening. And now Cooper always requested more information. He was sickened by the fact that he'd probably picked it up from one of the municipal board's endless meetings.

"Send it to the task force," Trevor said. This was a stinging rebuke. He'd heard Cooper vent about that phrase to Libby again and again. "Task is right," Cooper would rant, "but *force* is way off the mark."

It was at this point in the discussion, after the first overt sarcasm, an attack, when Libby would immediately address the level of discourse, allowing not one bit of disrespect. It leveled everyone. For some reason, Cooper had never felt it was his right to do this. He was going to stay in the ring and he was not going to lose his temper.

"Trevor, I just need to make a call. This"—he held up the potato gun—"is the unknown."

"Fine." His son held his hands aloft like a magician, showing he no longer had any hold over the current moment. "But get ready for what you're going to hear. The police are going to find out we've got potatoes, and besides that, tomatoes and those orange deals, carrots. You're opening the whole vegetable drawer to the government. You are unbelievable."

Libby came into the garage now. Trevor finished with "Good luck with it all," and crossed into the house.

Cooper's wife had the phone on her shoulder and her face was blanched. When he saw the phone he thought it was the planning office calling for his report, but then he knew, or afterward it felt like he knew. He gave her the potato gun and said, "Hold this," and then he put the telephone to his ear.

There was nothing to do. He had always been close to his mother, shared her word games and her wavelength of humor, and had known that so much of his work with the city was done so that when his name was in the paper, she could show her Scrabble buddies and e-mail his aunts. Now he called the aunts and went down to the hospital. He put his hand on her forehead, which was not cold, and they gave him a little bag with her wedding ring and her dentures and such. Cooper's father had already been gone fifteen years. His mother had called that morning. She was going to get a new dishwasher and asked Cooper what he thought of Days Appliance. He told her the store was where he and Libby had bought their fridge. She was doing her puzzle society newsletter and asked him which character in Shakespeare had the longest name. He didn't know, but guessed, "Rosencrantz? Eleven letters."

"Why did we send you to college?" she said. She always said this; it was their oldest joke. They made plans for the Thursday drive to the library, and when they hung up, she said, "There, I feel better."

In the quiet room in the hospital, using two phones, Cooper made the arrangements: transfer, cremation, memorial service on Friday. Then he drove home light to light, avoiding the 101, and near home he finally said it aloud, "Your mother is dead." His reaction was as he suspected; he didn't believe it. He tried to say it again and couldn't. At the house Libby came out to his car when she heard the garage door open. He got out and told her, "We're all right."

Trevor stood in the kitchen and gave Cooper a cursory hug, the way they'd always hugged. "Sorry about Grandma, Dad."

Cooper fought through the sympathy and got to his desk. He didn't even want a drink. He wrote the light-rail report in forty minutes, an ace job, which he faxed to the office after hours. In bed, Libby rolled to him and rubbed his back, but he felt hollow, and he held on to his pillow so he wouldn't float away.

In the morning with a pencil on the patio, Cooper wrote his mother's obituary, two short paragraphs in the customary manner, centering it with, "She had a head for puzzles and a heart for people." He wanted to write, "She sent me to college and never got to ride the train."

He wanted to write about all the people she had cared for. He'd grown up across the street from a ragtag sandlot, where all his buddies came to play ball. Afternoons in the summertime, his mother would sit out in the shadow of their house in a canvas lawn chair and do her cryptograms and puzzles and talk to his friends. It stunned him that he'd be out in center field and look over to see Danny Lopez or Robert Polad sitting on the lawn by her, just talking things over. At the various reunions he and Libby had gone to over the years, people always asked about his mother, and told him how important she had been to them.

While he was faxing the obituary to the newspaper, the phone rang and it was the mayor herself calling about the rail proposal. She loved it; they were going to use great portions in the ad campaign. "You're so good at this, Peter. Let's get together tomorrow for strategy. Now the fun begins." Then she added, "And I want to meet your mother. She sounds wonderful."

"She's something," he said.

Cooper had met his wife when they were in high school. He had been president of the Civics Club and a tall, quiet kid the teachers liked. He initiated a program wherein the club cleaned up bus stops, and he met Libby literally while painting a bench sky blue. They still knew the bench, the corner (as did Trevor, who used it in much of his humor), and they'd painted it twice in the last ten years, late at night both times, on their anniversary.

When they met, Libby had suggested they attend the fall dance, since the Civics Club was one of the sponsors. It had not occurred to Cooper to go to a dance. Girls had not actually occurred to Cooper. In the old gymnasium, where the decorating committee had made six bus stops around the perimeter with benches and lampposts, and a big blue cardboard bus circled the dancers, Cooper woke to his new world. Libby was a wry girl who wore a vintage brown silk dress run with a single line of black beads that climbed her in a spiral. She started their longtime game on that first night when she asked him if he knew what dancing was. Before them the shiny floor was filled with their classmates, embraced and shuffling to "Moon River."

"I don't know," he told her truly.

"It's a simple space-saving activity. See how neat they fit on the dance floor?"

He looked at her.

"Here," she went on. "It's like holding hands." She clasped his hand and lifted it before them. "See?" Then she threaded her fingers between his and he felt an actual naked shock. No one had touched him that way, but when she folded her hand shut on his, he did the same to her.

"Now we're saving space," she said. "Let's try to dance."

She came carefully into his arms for the first time, floating delicately against his tweed sport coat. "Moon River" was waning fast, but they stepped slowly in their little circle, her forehead just against his temple. The music stopped, and still they stood. He could feel the line of beads under his fingers. He knew something had happened because they did not move. When the small combo began the next number, "Chances Are," they danced further into the old gym.

Later, in college when he'd visit, they'd twist together on her roommate's couch, every adjustment meant to save space, and the second summer in a beach motel for some reason called Tumble Inn, in a bed that would have been a better hammock, she looked him in the eye as they made a last adjustment.

They were at schools four hundred miles apart and saw each other every weekend their senior year. In one letter, she said, "I feel at every moment that there is a good chance I am wasting space up here. Being engaged is a colossal waste of space! Where are you?"

After their first date, the fall dance, Cooper told Libby he was taking her to a small Italian place he knew. The custom was for couples to go to fancy restaurants after dances, and Cooper drove down Main Street for a while and then cut right for his house. His mother had a red-checked tablecloth on a round table in the basement and his father had melted candles into a Coke bottle, and the ambience was complete. Libby, of course, picked it up at once, and said she'd heard this place was the best Italian in the state.

"Which state is that?" his mother had said, and they'd started in laughing. Cooper, who had agreed to this dinner plan because he didn't exactly know the customs of his classmates, was slightly embarrassed; he was always slightly embarrassed. He watched Libby and his mother hit it off as if this had been their plan, and he felt that feeling he'd had when as a boy in center field he'd seen his friends sitting on his lawn, talking to his mother, and he knew for the first time, the feeling was a kind of happiness.

Condolence flowers started arriving the next day. Cooper worked at home in the morning and the doorbell rang every forty minutes. He had to go across town to the funeral home as a formality. The law required that he identify her there before the cremation. He used the thought to do all the ugly work on his desk, filing and turgid phone calls, stale business with his various clients, going down the list like a man cutting dry weeds with a scythe.

At the bottom of his sheet, he had written *Police*, and he couldn't figure it out for a moment. Then he looked up the local station number and dialed. A woman answered, Officer Betty Dodd, and he explained that this was no emergency, but that he just wanted some simple information on a potato gun; had she heard of potato guns?

"What kind of gun is this, sir?" Officer Dodd asked.

"It's a kind of a glorified toy; it shoots potatoes. Is there someone there who I could ask about it?"

"You're speaking to me," she said. "Is it a toy gun?"

"I don't know. My son has constructed this potato gun and—"

"Is this a school-sponsored project?"

"No, it's not," Cooper said, immediately wishing he'd said

yes, yes indeed. "It's just a home project that we're moving along with. It'll be fine. I'll call you back when we get close. Thank you for your assistance." He hung up the receiver. Cooper was an effusive thanker. When people told him to have a nice day, he thanked them. His mother always responded to "Have a nice day" with, "Shoot, I've got other plans."

In the kitchen Libby had her next semester's plan spread over the table in three-by-five cards. The red cards were music projects, the blue cards were lectures, and the white cards were rehearsals. She was a scrupulous planner, and after these years of teaching, she wrote each class as if inventing it. She was the mentor for the first-year teachers. "Do you want me to drive with you?" she asked her husband.

"No, I can make it. The traffic won't be bad." If he could keep it all business, he could handle it. There had been moments when his mother's death rushed him, and breath gone, he'd have to lean against something. This feeling of void was not in his vocabulary. The closest he could come was remembering when they'd taken nine-year-old Trevor to Hoover Dam, and walked the curved sidewalk along the top. There with the other citizens it looked like a promenade, the two art deco towers standing calmly in the massive blue lake. They ate ice cream and Trevor explained hydroelectricity. But Cooper couldn't help working to the other edge, leaning over the stone rail and having the deep gorge suck the blood out of his head until he saw spots. Then when he was back with his family, a dropped napkin was right there to be picked up, the sidewalk solid, his son's voice constant. Cooper thought, Behind me four feet is the true nothingness, but if I don't look, we'll make it across.

Now his mother's death was that open canyon, waiting to be considered, waiting for all of him. He rippled with a shudder, and shook it off. He wouldn't cry now. Libby stood him up with a hug, her lips against his cheek.

The phone rang and Libby answered with a puzzled look, handing it to Cooper. It was Sergeant Meager with the police. As soon as he said, "Mr. Cooper," Cooper stepped in the game. They had his name and number, for Pete's sakes. He was good at this, especially on the telephone. "Have you got some problem with a gun?"

"I'm sorry, Sergeant. What is it?"

"The referral says potato gun."

"Potato *bug*," Cooper said, his eyes on Libby. He was mad and now he'd stay controlled and win this. "I called a minute ago about these bugs. We have got a genuine infestation. But I also just called the etymologist at Natural Resources, and she's going to call me back." There was a pause on the line, and Cooper went on: "I told the receptionist——"

"Officer Dodd."

"I told Officer Dodd this wasn't an emergency. I sure appreciate you getting back to me, though. You don't have them, do you? I'm not even sure they're potato bugs. They may be this white bug or white fly, whatever it is."

"Have a nice day," Sergeant Meager said.

Cooper put the phone down and said to his wife, "Case closed."

The last time Cooper saw his mother was in a small curtained room near the back of the funeral home. She was swaddled in a white cotton blanket and looked comfortable. Her gray hair was combed straight back, which was a way she never wore it, but was the way that Cooper did, and he saw his face in her again. Her forehead was cool now, and he put his fingers on her cheek and said the word "Good-bye."

Cooper's 1956 Chevrolet was a four-door Bel Air like new. It was the actual car that his father had bought in the fall of 1955. It had been the family car, then Cooper had taken it to college. Later it was sold to a neighbor and gone for five years. Cooper's father had tracked it down in San Diego and restored the car, bit by bit.

Now Cooper pulled the cloth cover off the vehicle. He pushed it out of the garage and dusted it generally with his soft brush. He poured red fluid into the transmission; it always lost a little when parked for a month or two. The ignition key was worn smooth, but when he turned it, the car cranked twice and fired to life. He fed fuel for a moment and then let the vehicle settle into its purring idle. "Like a sewing machine," his father always said. While the engine warmed up, Cooper walked around the car with his cloth, dusting and polishing. The prom was in two hours.

Helping Trevor with the bow tie for his tux ten minutes before, Cooper had said, "This is a new record for ties in a week." He'd stood behind his son the day before and formed a Windsor knot in a blue stripe tie, which Trevor then pulled apart and redid, saying, "That's clever how it cinches." In one minute the boy had mastered ties. That tie had been for the memorial service, which had filled the little chapel. They had all been people his mother had talked to, counseled over the years, a collection of her puzzle buddies, the neighbors, her nieces and nephews. Cooper had given the eulogy, stepping through the stages of his mother's life by keeping his back to the canyon, not letting his mind look over the edge.

Now Trevor came out of the house walking stiffly in his tuxedo, carrying a little corsage in a plastic box with both hands.

The car was running beautifully. First they picked up Justin on the other side of the high school. Cooper tried to imagine where in the house they hid the potato gun, where they shot it. Justin got in the car and saw Trevor's corsage and ran back into the house for the one he'd forgotten.

Both girls, Alison and Deanie, were at Alison's house, and there was an extended photo session in the living room. The girls were in satin spaghetti-strapped gowns, one dark blue and one light blue, and the comedy of five parents, two corsages, and one little sister played for ten minutes before Cooper was able to ascertain that Alison was Trevor's date. She was a tall, beautiful girl, and with her brown hair up, she was taller than Trevor. She had a mole beside her nose that Cooper thought might have been makeup, a touch, and she wore large glasses that actually looked wonderful on her smooth face. There was some talk about the eyewear, Alison's mother admitting to Cooper that she could have contacts any time she wanted. To this Alison had smiled and said to Cooper, "Contacts? When I can wear these?"

Trevor was a little stiff, but it was clear he liked Alison's humor. He didn't exactly stand close to her for the photos, but she took his arm and pulled him over. Justin had snaked an arm around Deanie; this wasn't their first date.

When the kids finally boarded the car, all four slid into the backseat and Alison's father closed one door while Cooper closed the other.

"How skinny can they be?" Alison's mother laughed.

Cooper saluted and started the old Chevrolet.

They had dinner at Leonardo's Submarines, a tacky sandwich shop in a small strip mall by the hospital. Cooper opened the car doors, and though he told Libby he was going to disappear, not talk, be the driver, he had to ask, "Why here?"

Alison smiled and she and Deanie leaned their heads together to sing, "For your birthday or your prom, for your sister or your mom, for your every party plan, it's Leonardo's." It was a radio jingle, and it was vaguely familiar.

The girls laughed. "It's our prom," Deanie said. "We promised we'd come here for the junior prom."

Trevor smiled at Cooper and shrugged. "It's a cheap date." The two couples turned and strode like royalty into the little shop. Cooper could see the red-checked tablecloths through the window, and a number of people turned to see who was coming in the door. How would he know a cheap date, Cooper thought, he's never been on a date.

He closed the car doors again and felt the sickening pull of the abyss. Everything was normal here, he needed not to look over.

The prom was at the Tamarisk Country Club, way north in the desert. When Cooper had picked the foursome up at Leonardo's, they were all talking, spirited, and he found himself invisible. It was the last minute of twilight in the high desert. In the backseat the kids talked over one another about Jackson Pollock, Kelvin temperatures, and the phrase "No Fear." Justin was evidently an expert on things and started his sentences with, "In reality . . ." and "The fact is . . ." Alison had a funny bit, which she'd pull out every few minutes when it would get quiet: "If you don't understand," she'd say, "then raise your hand." In the rearview, Cooper could see them all raise their hand every time and then laugh.

The sprawling pink-roofed developments dropped behind, and Cooper drove up through the undulating desert shelf. Set alone at the foot of the darkening McDowell Mountains, the Tamarisk Country Club looked like a madman's fortress surrounded by a golf course. The huge circular drive was flagstone lined with the magnificent desert trees, and when Cooper pulled up to the red carpet entry, the valets, eight kids in white satin jackets glowing in the new dark, ran to his door.

"It's just a dropoff," he told them as he opened the door and the four beautiful young people slid out.

"Is this a 'fifty-five?" one of the valets asked.

" 'Fifty-six," he told him.

"What a sweet car," another said. Trevor was already marching off a step ahead of Alison along the lighted walk toward the stone-and-glass edifice of the Tamarisk. He saw her catch him and take his arm. Just before they entered the massive wooden doors, he saw them all raise their hands.

Now the dark came up for him, and turning down the broad alluvial slope, he could see the city below, beds of dotted lights layered to the world's edge. There was still one band of dark blue along the horizon like the edge of a serrated knife. He turned on the old radio, AM only, with the two civil defense triangles on the lighted dial. It took a moment and then another to warm up and then it was Ricky Nelson singing "Traveling Man" on KOY, the vintage station he always kept the radio tuned to as a joke, as if the music were coming across the decades. The tune, touring the women of the world, prefigured "California Girls." Cooper liked the line "my sweet fraulein in Berlin Town." The wind in the windows helped, but he could taste the vertigo again, the pull.

At home, Libby had the table set. She was going to put out a midnight buffet for the kids. She put her hands on Cooper's chest and saw his face. "Come on," she told him. "Open this." She handed him a cold bottle of champagne. "You can have one drink. You've got three hours before duty."

She poured the wine into two of her big white coffee cups from school and led Cooper out into the backyard. As always, there was a lawn chair on the bottom of their swimming pool. It was where Trevor sat when he was out here. He had a set of rubber-coated hand weights, and he used them to walk around the bottom and sit in the chair. Cooper and his wife sat in the old cushion swing and looked down into the grassy common, which gave onto the rocky wash that ran diagonally through the district.

Cooper knew he should say something. He knew she was worried about him, but he couldn't move a single word forward. He was stilled and growing brittle. He could feel his mother's forehead now, and he turned fully to the lip of Hoover Dam and he leaned into the waiting white emptiness as it rose to meet him. His breath was gone and he was falling. There was nothing. Libby took his hand, wove her fingers through his and squeezed. "Hold on," she whispered, and gravity returned as her arm went around his shoulder and he felt the first tear hit his shirt. "Look," she said. Cooper opened his eyes and saw the narrow shape of a coyote on the far side of the pool, drinking silently. Another snout appeared from the dark and dipped to the water. Both animals were focused on the two people on the swinging bench, and then the coyotes vanished. Cooper blinked his eyes and checked. Gone.

"I loved her, too," Libby said.

Cooper nodded. He could nod.

Libby put Cooper's cup on the little redwood table. "Come on, mister. Let's go in. What are we doing out here? Our son is at the prom. We could save some space."

What was it like in the bed? Physical therapy? Something. Libby helped him with his clothes and moved upon him, placing his leg so, his arms, turning him, talking softly all the while, and then he kindled, claiming himself as he came to life, clashing with her body and her intent, working against her, with her, until the man made of stone was human again in these efforts. At one point, she smiled up at him and said, "Well, there you are."

A moment later, he said to her, "Here I am. I was busy for a minute."

"We can sleep for a while now," Libby said. "I'll wake you at eleven." She kissed him and wouldn't let him roll away, rolling with him, and she was there on his back as he crossed the line into sleep.

His dream was a variation of the old dream: he was floating up without any support and the view was special, the houses, businesses, and streets, but he couldn't control his speed or direction and he wanted down. He was always a little higher than it was safe to be. Then he saw his mother. Without transition, he was in a dark hallway of an old school, and passing a classroom window he saw her in the class, which must have been a typing class, because each student sat before an old typewriter. There was an expression on her face, a quiet smile, that let him know she knew he was at the window, but she would not turn to him. He was late for something and passed by, stunned by the last thing: she'd had a suntan. She looked about forty and healthy; she'd been working in the garden?

Cooper drove behind the Tamarisk Country Club and parked in one of the three ranks of limousines. The parking lot lay against the dark mountain. There was an archway of balloons coming out of the club, lined with tables where volunteers were giving keepsakes to the departing promgoers. Cooper couldn't shake the classroom scene from his dream. It made him smile. He got out into the warm night and opened his trunk. The music pulsed through the trees, something Cooper almost recognized. He thought these things were all thrash, crash, and hip hop. The musical measures he could grasp now evaporated before he could name them, but some part of it was old, some rock melody. He could see two couples on the terrace, two hundred yards off, leaning in tight, passionate twists, making out. Saving space early.

The old Chevrolet was sparkling, but he polished the corner of the bumpers, under the brow of the headlights, the door handles. The limo driver ahead of him sauntered back smoking a cigarette. He held up his cell phone and said, "It was ten-thirty, then eleven-thirty, now twelve. It must be a good dance."

"They call you from inside?" Cooper asked the man.

"It goes up to the satellite and then straight down to me, so the kid can do the tango right over there." The driver waved his hand at Cooper's car. "We had a 'fifty-six, two-door. It was that black and white, remember that one?"

"I do. They had a red and white, a blue and white, and the two-tone green."

"That was a weird one. Avocado and tan? I wish I still had ours. It could go. Has this got the 283?"

"Right," Cooper said. "It wants to go." He opened the hood and the limo driver marveled at how simple the setup was.

"You could work on a car like this." The driver had taken his cap off and leaned over the red engine block, the shiny hoses. "My old man wasn't happy unless he was under the hood every weekend. What was he doing?"

"Getting it right," Cooper said.

Couples had begun to emerge from the country club, some of the girls carrying their shoes. "Here we go," the driver said.

"Where you taking them now?" Cooper asked him.

"These six young people are going to the Hyatt for the night, after they pay me an hour and a half extra. You take care." He snugged on his cap and went down to his vehicle and opened all the doors.

A minute later, Trevor appeared under the balloons, strolling as if on tour alone, and then Cooper saw a hand take his arm and Alison pulled herself into view. She was still smiling; that was a good sign. They accepted a gift from the table and stepped down into the parking lot. Behind them two or three couples came the duet of Deanie and Justin, wrapped together like fate itself.

After the kids had grazed Libby's buffet, Cooper made himself a big sandwich on the fresh sourdough bread, putting a slice of everything in it. The girls were filling Libby in on what everyone wore. The gifts had turned out to be small silver frames with the prom picture already in there—a Polaroid, Cooper guessed: his son in a tuxedo under an arbor beside a beautiful young woman. This year Trevor's eyebrows had grown together and Cooper had asked his wife if he (meaning she) should mention it. She had said, "No, as soon as they pluck that eyebrow, it's all over." He looked carefully at the little picture. His son had two eyebrows.

He hauled his sandwich out into the backyard and washed it down with sips of warm champagne as he watched the two couples talk to his wife in the lighted kitchen. Evidently Justin could eat, talk, and still keep his eyes on Deanie's cleavage, such as it was. Suddenly they all stood up and filled the room, such tall people, and they filed into the laundry room for the garage.

Cooper found them admiring the potato gun. Libby was offering the party line about Cooper finding out the legalities, when Cooper spoke. "Let's test it right now, Mrs. Cooper. Have you any potatoes?"

"Yes I do."

"Well, Trevor, get your gear and let's go."

They drove in the Chevrolet, Libby now with him in the front seat, out through the narrow piece of the reservation and across the canal at the Surplus Bridge. Cooper directed Justin to open the state land gate, and suddenly they were in the raw desert and the smell of creosote and juniper flooded the car. At twenty miles an hour, Cooper turned off his lights and drove another ten minutes on the dirt track, the young people quieted by the looming paloverdes and ocotillos reaching for the car.

"Looks good to me," Cooper said.

There was no moon, but the desert floor glowed as they all stepped out of the car. "Are you sure, Dad?" Trevor said.

"Absolutely," Cooper answered. "Justin, where do you shoot yours?"

"My dad won't let me finish it," Justin said. He had his arm around Deanie again. "We're never going to shoot it."

Cooper looked at the boy.

There was a noise down the road and Cooper reached in and pulled on the headlights. They all saw a pig step onto the road, unhurried, and then five more javelinas came out, picking at the sweetgrass along the rutted dirt path. "Wow," whispered Alison, "look." Libby came against Cooper and took his arm. More of the animals emerged, a dozen, then more, big and small, some babies trotting comically behind the pack. They were all starting and stopping, rooting and bumping, as they crossed the road. A midsize pig trotted up and mounted one of the females who had stopped to eat, and he humped on her casually amid the grouping. "Uh-oh," Deanie said, and all four of the young people raised their hands and laughed. The laughter didn't hurry the javelina troop at all, but Cooper pushed the lights off, saying, "They don't need this," and soon the pigs were gone.

"Are you all set?" he asked Trevor.

"When you are."

Cooper had everyone stand behind Trevor, and the boy in his tuxedo trimmed a potato and rammed it into the barrel. He charged the chamber with a touch of butane and, holding it aloft, touched the end with the automatic match. The noise was a two-part *wa-whump!* and they all strained their eyes at the night sky. Trevor, careful to keep the barrel pointed away, turned to them and said, "Sweet."

"Victory is ours," Cooper said.

"How far did it go?" Justin asked.

Trevor fired it four more times and then Cooper drew a line in the sand with a stick. "I'll go straight out the road," Cooper said. "When I wave my arms, I'll be at a hundred yards. Fire straight so I can measure." He was ready to step it off when there was a hand at his sleeve: Alison.

"Trevor told me about his grandmother. I'm sorry for your loss."

"I appreciate that," he told the girl. Then Cooper marched down the white-sand road in the desert night counting his steps. At one hundred he dragged a line across the road with his heel. He turned and could see Trevor's tuxedo shirt glowing near the shiny top of the car. Everything else was dark forms. Around him, Cooper could hear rustling in the ditches.

He heard the two-part concussion and saw the potato tumbling over his head at the same time. It hit the road and exploded. He stepped it off: seventeen more yards. He waved the rag again. This time the potato veered left and crashed into the trees. Cooper waved again. For a while that was what they did late in the night and into the early hours after the junior prom. Cooper was laughing as his son shot potatoes into the desert. The longest straight measure was 123 yards. When he finally put his rag in his pocket, Cooper could hear the pigs working hard through the brush for these succulent wonders.

GARY GARRISON'S WEDDING VOWS

GARY GARRISON GAVE RADCLIFFE a second try, but when she came home to New York having completed her sophomore spring, she announced that her academic career was over. "It isn't a good idea for me to be up there cutting classes to sit around my room having feelings," she told her mother. The classes were excellent, if large, but all they inspired in her were feelings. She took differential calculus and got feelings. She took philosophy and got feelings. She took Advanced French and The American Renaissance and they gave her feelings. She walked the campus and through the town at odd hours, driven by emotions she could not control, an urgent sense of the size and magnitude of all knowledge. She would sit in her room and feel her emotions surge in her like an uproarious tide anxious on a steep rocky shore. Gary made the actual decision to let go of college while perched in a tree on the quad. She entered the thick umbrella of an ancient pine and then climbed the puzzling and ready ladder of limbs around its trunk until she was two hundred feet from the ground and could see the lights of Boston. She was twenty years old.

"I am destined to go through life as an exposed nerve," she said. "That's what I learned at college. I hope you don't feel I wasted your fifty thousand dollars. The food was good."

"You're going to be fine, Margaret," her mother told her.

"You're the kind of girl who will look out the window while you talk to people. You are high strung, but you won't perish. It will make you a good listener. Your life is going to be lovely if you can find the right company."

Gary was looking out the window now and she turned to her mother, defiant and understood. She sat with the fingertips of her left hand touching the fingertips of her right hand, a posture of power and fragility at once. "I'm going to get a job," she said. "And try to grow some insulation." She didn't know what to do about being the kind of person who was driven by emotion, who climbed trees, whose eyes watered three or four times a day from a feeling she could only take as happiness. She saw meaning everywhere but couldn't interpret it, and this made her alert, constantly, for signals from the world. Some people viewed her as superstitious and overly sensitive, but everyone saw her as charming, for she represented a stage they'd all known but could not sustain, a dear wakefulness that had in them subsided.

For these reasons no one was surprised a year later to hear of the shape of the nuptials she had fashioned, the conditions, how the whole wedding would work. She was a lifetime away, in Utah, and was marrying, if all things came to pass, a successful lawyer who chaired the board of the bird sanctuary where she'd taken work. The ceremony was being held in a little church north of the village of Brigham City, a building that looked like a child's drawing of a church, and it stood among cornfields there. The wedding would commence at the moment of sunset on December 10, and the only light would be the twelve candles, one on each windowsill of the plain building, and there would be no spoken "I do's." In her time west, Gary Garrison had learned to love geese, and had had moments when she felt she understood what they were saying, was sure of it, not as something she could translate but as something she could feel. The large wild birds affected her.

The wedding vows would be read in the candlelit church, and then Gary Garrison and her husband-to-be, William Brookes, would stand with the minister until they heard the call of geese. The call of the geese would seal the deal. In the invitation it said it this way: "When the wild geese call, we will be married heart and soul, and only **IF** they call."

Her mother smiled to read the invitation, imagining Gary's new life in the larger world, seeing a hundred wedding guests in the dark room listening for the winging birds.

After leaving college, Gary Garrison went west to wear out her feelings, but it didn't happen that way. She traveled by car and all the new places gave her feelings, fresh electricity every morning, noon, and night. Times, many times, she pulled off the interstate onto some back road and stood, arms folded, against her car, breathing deeply and trying not to cry. Traveling this way, by fits and starts, she arrived in Utah and took the job a friend of her father's had arranged at the Brigham Bird Refuge.

"She wants out of doors," her father had said. "We'll arrange it."

There her story began, for she fell under the spell of the sky and a man. It was September, which offered up a crazy fragile blue, a season of crumbling summer and its crushing light, light about to fall off a polished table like a crystal vase, light that filled Margaret Garrison like fire in a bowl, and in her September days, she walked upon her toes to get her head up into the air as far as possible.

Where she walked upon her toes was along the causeways that formed a large grid through the wetlands well north of the giant Great Salt Lake. These were little more than gravel dikes grown with reeds and marked by the single trail where the manager of the refuge and his minions marched. On such a narrow path, with water on both sides in great blue-sky sheets, she felt herself drift away more than once. What she had in her hand was a notebook with a green canvas cover, and inside the cover on the lined pages of the thing were two types of entry. One was the bird count at each station, along with the time and the date and one-line descriptions of any birds she did not recognize, exotic ducks or the like. The other entry in Margaret's official book was her poetry. The back of her book began to thicken with blue pages of her free verse, written, like so many things she did, because she could not not do it. If she did not write the poetry when she sat alone in the barrel blinds and on the platforms watching ducks settle and feed, she would not have burst or had a breakdown, but some small gasket in her would have surely cracked.

It was as if she were born for the task of learning birds, for their names came to her immediately, and she could distinguish them by their profiles in the sky at some distance and by the way they sat on the water or landed, and she knew the various geese and ducks by their calls of succor and distress, and her notebook thickened with her fall census.

The manager of this private wetland was a trained wildlife ranger named Mark Faberhand, who was thirty-one years old and had become at that age a flinty expert in the western flyways and in all birds, even exotics. He was tall and permanently tanned and taciturn, and he struck people on first meeting as being furry, for he shaved once a week on Sunday. His role had evolved on the thousand acres of the refuge to that of policeman really, and he had grown into that part reluctantly, even though it was what he did. He'd pull up to the pickups full of scouting hunters or young lovers or older lovers who were off from their lawful spouses, and he'd step to their vehicles in his green refuge uniform with his flashlight and he'd ask them to move on. The hunters would kid with him, pleading, Come on, you've got so many Canadian honkers, share a few, scare some over this way.

The skies were busy all September and that doubled in October, the steady migration of waterfowl loading the morning and evening with sublime traffic. No day or part of a day was lost to Gary Garrison. She was out early, five A.M., walking the reedy pathways in the chilly dark to count the incoming ducks and outgoing ducks, and she learned to tell by the way some took off that they were actually going off to feed and would stay another day. The first thing she heard every day in the sky was the whistling wings of the low-flying, fast-flying ducks, and the last thing she heard at the sharp edge of the short fall twilight was the honking of the Canadian geese as they settled.

The geese became her favorite, and their cries felt personal to her and at the same time part of some larger fate, tied to the vastness of the sheeted waterlands and the mountains as they flared and faded. The geese in their afternoon squadrons, arriving or departing or crossing high overhead, seemed part of a force that she longed for, and that is why they figured later in her wedding plans. When the time came, they would perform the ceremony.

The other intern in the wetland sanctuary that fall was Juanita Dubois, a young woman who had recently graduated from Utah State University with a degree in wildlife management. Juanita already had been hired by the State of Utah, and she would be working the Central Wildlife District starting in the spring. The two women roomed together in a new trailer across the gravel yard from the one permanent structure on the grounds, the administration cabin. Three days a week the women went together in the refuge truck to six ponds in rotation, and their census involved a check sheet of time of day, water temperature, bird count, etcetera. Every Friday, they met with Mark Faberhand in the little cabin, entered data, and planned the coming week. It was a regulated pattern that fall, but in her heart as always Gary Garrison felt as if she had a secret that was ineffable, unspeakable, that it filled her and emptied her like a bellows. Mornings when the first wings would whistle overhead in the starry black, she'd gasp and sit down and feel the water burn to the surface of her eyes.

She wrote to her mother: "I will not climb a tree and quit this place! There are no trees, and simply this has claimed me, incurably. Not curable. Incurably incurable! There's no cure for this love, if that is what it is. I love the sun, the mud, the traveling birds too much!"

Juanita Dubois was a level-headed, steady friend for Gary. She was smart and energetic and plainspoken. She was annoyed to have done so well in her classes at Utah State that she'd scared away possible boyfriends, and in the evenings while Gary lay in her bunk and listened to every living thing moving in the sky, Juanita listed each man she'd almost dated. Her admiration for Mark Faberhand was immediate and complete, and over the weeks of the fall, it crossed over to affection, which she also reported to Gary Garrison in their night quarters.

With Mark, on their forays in the field and at their weekly meetings, Gary kept quiet. She also admired many things about him, but she didn't think about them, because she saw they would never end. The list would start with his speaking voice and move from the hair on his wrists to his walk in his heavy brown lace-up boots and to his general ethic, and she didn't know how to control such a list or the feelings it engendered. He was a good man, and she hadn't known any. Being around him vexed her because it was like interference; she could feel him there more clearly than the outer world. The only time she was surprised by incoming flights or ducks in the reeds was when she was out with him. She also understood her feelings because she could never face him full on, turn to him openly, even to stand and talk. She kept to one side, nodded his way, and spoke looking past his shoulder the way she'd seen baseball coaches talk to pitchers on the mound.

When she was out alone that fall, she thought she might die of the beauty or whatever it was about this wild world. And then she thought that double because each day was shorter than the one before and each day there were fewer birds, as the thousands of wildfowl rested and then went on toward Mexico.

Some days the three of them came across trespassers and had to intervene. Mark would stand out of the truck with Juanita behind him while whoever had camped on the property packed up their gear and drove off. A couple of times Mark had Juanita walk up to a pickup on one of the dirt access roads and say, "Listen, boys, you're going to have to move on. The property line is a half mile back."

"You the bird woman?"

"I am Officer Dubois, the citation person." And she'd reach into her back pocket for her ticket book. "And who are you?" She lifted her pen. "Or were you leaving?"

At such moments, Gary would watch Mark smile at the proceedings, and she could feel static across the top of her heart. He was slow to smile and a smile made his face a wonder.

Juanita would stride back to their truck and say, "In the line of duty, from time to time, there is no better posture for a conservation officer than to be a hard-ass." She'd salute Mark and move past him to get in the vehicle.

———

"Where does he live?" Juanita asked that night. "Is he married?" But she didn't wait for answers; she was building a solid theory on the evidence. "His lunches, in my opinion, are not made by a woman. I haven't seen anything in those thick sandwiches except packaged cheese and salami. And he's using that same brown paper bag four, five days in a row. I haven't seen a napkin or a treat large or small."

Gary agreed with all of this and could have taken it a step further because she'd had half of one of Mark's homemade sandwiches a day or so before, and it had sandwich spread inside, too, something made of Thousand Island dressing and pickles, which she had never tasted before in her life. Since he had handed her the sandwich, she had not been able to think to the end of a sentence. His fingerprints were in the bread, and when she put her teeth into the thing, she was changed and she knew it.

"I figure his heart got broken when he was up in Missoula at school," Juanita continued, "and he's been out here for six years, living in a basement apartment in Brigham, oiling his boots and ironing his own shirts. He's pretty good at it. He doesn't go out much. He's afraid of love. Hasn't met the right woman." Juanita was silent a moment. "Until now."

"You go on the count tomorrow," Gary said to her friend. "I'll lay in. I could use the sleep."

"Are you okay? Do you feel sick?"

"Juanita," she said. "I'll sleep in tomorrow. Say hello to all my babies. And be nice to Mark." But in the morning as soon as Juanita left, Gary dressed and sat in the chilly morning on a folding chair in the trailer yard and watched the light come. Her thoughts changed channels for hours.

When she'd been out with Mark alone, they didn't talk. He wasn't a talker and she said nothing, afraid that if she ever started, she could not restrain any of the words, the feelings that rose in her. So they sat in one of the large barrel blinds and watched the geese. They were so close that every breath, every small movement and shift seemed like code. At one point she saw him tilt his head to look closer at something and his mouth opened, and when his lips parted, she heard the sound they made, they were that close. A group of a dozen Canadian geese came from the north and went behind them when suddenly Mark put his hand on Gary's shoulder and nodded before making a sharp barking noise, two loud syllables she recognized as the honking of geese. His hand on her shoulder emptied her head and she focused, such a relief. He called again, honking, and then three more in succession. He nodded his head again, and she saw the flock turning toward them, calling. They circled past and then came back in a splashing assault on the pond where Mark and Gary hid in their barrel. A moment ago they had been at eight hundred feet, and now they swam and settled in the dusk, twenty feet away. When Mark lifted his hand from her, Gary felt dizzy.

The big deal of the fall was the Trustee Tour and Dinner. The annual event was key to fund-raising for the year, and it was held the week before Halloween, when the foothills of the Wasatch were patched with gold and maroon, every orchard gone orange and rust, and the giant yellow cottonwoods dotting the hillsides. The desperate world was magnified, and Gary Garrison couldn't take a step without feeling the blue and the straw, the ivory and green burning in tiers up the graduated and massive slopes. The first snow had already cut triangles in the tops of the steely peaks. One noon two catering trucks came out into the refuge's dooryard and set up tables and lamps and portable heaters and a bar for cocktails.

It was in this circus of color at the high center of the last season of the year that she met William Bloom, the head of the trustees, a young attorney from Laramie, and their meeting, by torchlight in the open air of Utah, led to all the rest.

He saw her right away when the assemblage disembarked from the four blue vans that had delivered them from Salt Lake City. Within a minute he had taken in her carriage, the elevation of her face, her easy confidence, and he was a goner. He was thirty-two and had never felt anything like his awe and yearning for the young woman. Mark Faberhand led them out the primary embankment just as the sun set, and the fifty important personages, casting shadows that stretched a quarter mile onto the shallow ponds, watched the birds cross and recross the sky, settling, seeking shelter, and calling. Mark answered questions, as did Juanita and Gary, all dressed in their refuge uniforms, pressed and perfect. Back at the open-air dinner, William delivered remarks about the importance of the mission of the refuge, which made disciples of everyone at the long table. It was the best speech of his career.

Mr. Bloom was back the following afternoon in a plaid shirt and Levi's. Gary Garrison had never been courted before. There had been some boyfriends, but they were just that, boys. Everyone assumed a person of her beauty and idiosyncratic demeanor had a complete life, chapter and verse, and she was let alone. When she had received flowers, they were from her mother. William Bloom drove her to the Old Mill, the fanciest restaurant in the county, where the waiters wore lederhosen and green felt hats and stepped heavily around the wooden-floored room. William Bloom called her Margaret, which she didn't correct, because with all this new noise she felt like someone else.

After dinner he drove above one of the apple orchards, the trees all bright wrecks in the moonlight, and he pointed out the deer moving through the scrub oak. Deer that should have undermined her ability to breathe, sit still, but she watched the small herd move through from a new distance. Her mind on Mark and now William in her face, the smell of this big new car, a night plucked and stolen from the continuity of her electric life. He talked, a man's voice this close, about how much he loved the West, his life, the air, the dark, the mountains, etcetera, an unending inventory which she heard and after half an hour began to trust. His sincerity walled her in. He leaned to her and tried to kiss her and kissed her and still tried. A man's lips on her own crushed the circuits, and she kissed him back. He professed his love for her, apologized for saying it, and said it again. He drove her back to the refuge, stopping every fourth mile to kiss her and apologize.

In the trailer, Juanita waited until Gary sat on the bunk to say, "Mark came by to ask where you had gone to."

Gary was in hard flux and looked across the dark space to Juanita on an elbow on her cot. "And I told him, since he was so interested and has never asked you where I go when I drive to town to do the laundry and see a movie alone, that you were on a date with the king of this place."

"Don't be upset, Juanita."

"I'm not. Or maybe I am, but it's okay. Mark asks about you while you're out with William. It's strange for me. Envy rises from some deep pit. Oh well, I say, you get all the men, I get southern Utah this spring. It's a tough call."

When Gary saw Mark a few days later, he had already closed himself up like a resort town in winter.

William Bloom did not return to Laramie and his practice; he stayed on in Brigham City and pressed his suit with Gary. The days shortened, the sun like a weak flare rising and then the brief afternoons like an invitation to the brittle wind. The reeds along the ponds stiffened and there was lacy ice every morning. Walking back to the trailer in the broken light at day's end, Gary was as confused as she'd ever been. William's Land Cruiser idled in the yard.

They ate at the Old Mill three more times, saw two movies, ate at his hotel, necked in his room until every time he sat up and stopped them, placing his forehead against hers. He was in. He wanted something larger than sex in November in northern Utah. He said it to her that way and then asked her to marry him, come to Laramie. She told him she'd have to think. She needed a week.

It was late in the year now and the census told the story; every day fewer birds, and a magnificent golden loneliness fell upon Gary Garrison as she walked the embankments of the sanctuary. And every evening the day dropped away sharper and the few birds still called.

One afternoon at four o'clock, she sat on a levy with her notebook, her mind splintered. She wanted to sleep with William now, and she wanted to talk to Mark, who had shown her the power of this place, and she wanted no men at all, just a year of these creatures flying and calling. The sun rolled from east to west and the birds flew from north to south. It felt like the sky was being asked too much; it seemed that she was being asked too much.

It was then she heard the geese, a string of seven, calling in approach. She sat down in the dry reeds, and she put her head in her hands and sat still. She listened as their calling came louder and louder, her feet nearly in the icy water, and she wept without moving. When she peeked between her fingers again, the seven geese were settling at her feet. She could see the grain of the fine feathers on their necks and the glistening black center of each eye.

The large birds looked at her without remark, and she

knew what she was going to do, and that she would schedule the wedding at four o'clock, and like everything she had done so far, there would be an *if* in it. *If* the geese called, *so be it until death do us part.*

Gary's mother flew out a week early and in the hotel said, "I'm not surprised. I cannot be your mother and pretend to be surprised. It is sudden and strange, but he is a fine young man, and marriage might redirect the voltage in you. I'm an optimist."

Eighty-five people attended the little wedding north of Brigham City, two dozen of Gary's friends from New York and a few from college, her parents and her aunts, and a handful of her parents' friends. William Bloom's family, friends, and many of his associates from the greater West came to Utah for the event, happy for him, and curious about what they'd read on the invitation. They almost filled the wooden pews in the old church as they sat in the dusk, many watching the candles struggle in the leaky window boxes.

William Bloom looked like every young man looks when he gets married, serious and pretty, and those who knew him could see him breathing.

Margaret Garrison came up the aisle on her father's arm while one of her friends played "Segovia" on a big Gibson guitar, and the minister, a former state senator of Wyoming and a close family friend of the Blooms', read the sheets that Gary and William had created. It was noted that this was an unusual ceremony, but that marriage sometimes required the unusual, and that there were forces beyond this room, beyond this moment, forces that understood the world perhaps better than we do. Geese mate for life and travel together, and that was the intention in this bonding. "And so we agree and know that if we hear now the call of the wild geese, then Margaret and William will be man and wife." Then it grew quiet in the darkening church, and it stayed quiet as the candles worked against the larger night.

Juanita Dubois had done what she was to do at the appointed hour, that is, drive the refuge truck out to the stubble field on the high end of the wetland. But when she arrived there meaning to stir up the two dozen Canadian honkers who had been loitering for weeks, and who came and went with a casualness that made it seem they might try to stay all winter, they were gone. They were all gone. There were none, not a single goose.

Juanita checked her watch. It was nine minutes after four. She had her red satin dress hitched up to her knees and she was wearing her work boots unlaced. Her pumps were in the truck. She went to the far ditch and shined her mighty flashlight through the field. There was a last ribbon of green light in the west.

She found Mark Faberhand at the Clock Café on Main Street at 4:20 P.M. He had just ordered the hot roast beef sandwich and was folding the menu up when she came in. To her credit, she did not run in and grab him by the collar. "Juanita," he said. "What is it?"

The café light was bracing and full of hope, and she took a breath. "It's Gary. Do you think you could help us out?"

A quarter mile from the little church north of Brigham City, Utah, is a park that gives onto an open field that is sometimes winter wheat, sometimes alfalfa, many years simply volunteer growth of any kind, and Juanita parked the truck there as Mark had instructed her. The wind was at their back, blowing toward the building. They could see the candles in the windows.

"They've got candles in the windows," he said.

"They do," Juanita said.

Mark had a bottle of George Dickel in the truck and he

leaned against the grille of the vehicle for the engine warmth, and he took a slug of the whiskey and offered the bottle to Juanita.

"I'll have some," she said, and she tipped the bottle back. She kept having to finger the hair away from her face. "You don't have to do this," Juanita said. "If you want me to just take you back, I'll do it."

"No," he said. "Season's over. We'll take in the dock and lower the water this week. It's been a fall."

"You want me to put my arm around you?" she asked him.

"I do," he said. "I appreciate it." They stood side by side in the dark. "How long they been waiting?"

Juanita looked at her watch. "Thirty minutes."

"That's a long time to stand there. This is going to be the last singleton of the season, coming in late from somewhere." The he stood and cupped the side of his mouth with one hand and made the call, the two-part song of the Canadian goose in a rhythm he'd learned from the geese: one, four, then two, repeating one, four, and two. Then he did two and took a sharp sip from the bottle. "They're married now," he said. "That's got to serve."

All Gary Garrison heard was the first call, because by the second everyone was applauding and gasping and crying out, but it was all she needed to hear. She knew all about it, and she raised her finger for the ring.

AT THE EL SOL

I WAS STAYING AT THE El Sol on Durrant Street in Globe, Arizona, all of October, and it never cooled down. Mornings, when I was done with my assignment, I'd walk down to the Blue Door and have coffee and two poached eggs. This would have me walking back just before eleven, and most days Mr. Cuppertino would wave me into the little office, and we'd watch *The Price Is Right*. Mr. Cuppertino, whose wife had died that summer, loved *The Price Is Right* and he loved Bob Barker, the longtime host, who was exactly his age to the week, and he loved Roberta Gilstrand, who was one of the prize girls on the show, the brunette. We'd prop the door open and watch the color Zenith as the day heated up.

Afternoons I sat out in the metal lawn chair on the walkway in the shade and watched as the El Sol filled for the night. The folks who stopped at this motel were not on vacation; they were on other missions. As was I. If you left Los Angeles at six A.M. and you didn't boil over or ruin a tire up and over the Mohave, then you'd run through Phoenix in the midafternoon and be more than ready to shut it all down in Globe. And if you were on a bare budget like the ranchers and the roughnecks and the runaways who parked their dirty vehicles in the little paved courtyard as I sat and watched, the El Sol was a welcome oasis. It was a welcome oasis for me.

I was the only permanent resident, so to speak. I'd paid Mr.

Cuppertino three hundred dollars for the month, and I told him there might be a chance I'd be staying longer. I had almost nine hundred dollars of my own money, my personal gear, and the $5,100 from the casino scam. I had that money in a bag stuffed into my old watchman's jacket sleeve, hung with my stuff in the closet of Unit 7 of the El Sol.

Some afternoons Mr. Cuppertino would come out between arrivals and sit by me, and he told me about the various changes the place had seen under his hand. There had been an old swimming pool in the center of the courtyard which was now a patch of grass. It had been nothing but trouble. He told me the years and the colors he'd painted the place, red, turquoise, and the tan it was now. He showed me places on the old metal chairs in which we sat where those layers could be seen in the scratches. He'd been at the El Sol forty-five years and now his wife was dead and he wondered why even bother. A car would pull under the metal shade canopy off the office and Mr. Cuppertino would push himself out of the chair and say, "I'll go over and get my thirty-two bucks from these folks and be right back."

He had asked me what I was between, was I married, where was I headed, but I'd ducked most of it saying I was taking some time before heading home to Montana. I made the Montana part up; I just wanted someplace cold that would be understandable to avoid. But I also realized I made the home part up, too, because sitting there at the El Sol was pretty much it for me. My bridges were burned and reburned, and I was fairly sure in my scared little heart that those fires would eventually come for me, too.

What I was really doing was handwriting one complete chronological record of the five-week scam by which my associates and I had stolen $5,100 from the River of Gold Casino outside Incon, New Mexico. I was working on this project from early in the morning dark until about nine or so; I could only stand to work on the thing in the morning. I had a packet of notes I'd made on envelopes before I even knew what I was going to do with them, and my leaky memory, warped as it was by my love for that woman. I'd sit in the morning dark and write down in my new green spiral notebook everything that happened on September 5 and then everything that was said or done on September 6 and then where we were and how the plan evolved on each of the days, which were still so alive in my mind. So alive that it upset me to write them, yet I had to write them. I could never do a complete day in a morning. I kept thinking that I was working too slow, but it was the only way I could continue. Every time I mentioned someone, I wrote out the full name, such as Leo Rosemont or Baby Grayson, and when I came to my name I wrote it out full, too. I quoted what they said and what they were wearing. By the end of October at the El Sol I was halfway through September.

I needed to document what had happened and who had done wrong, while I could still remember when things had happened and who had said what. My head was ringing with these things, and I was setting them down in ink in my notebook to quiet myself down. I had a thick Shaeffer fountain pen and two bottles of brown ink, and the pages swelled under my writing. The days were filled with the sense that I would soon see a county cruiser in front of my room, and I would be certainly arrested. However, I also knew that the cruiser would be the best of the two things that could happen. The other would be Leo Rosemont himself rapping softly on the red motel door with the handle of his old revolver.

My first entry was dated September 4: I, Eugene Miner, was bit by a dog at the Statecore Refinery and quit that job. Driving up Incon Canyon north toward the summit, I met Baby Grayson, who had car trouble. She was headed south.

The next entry, dated September 5, takes off from right there because it had been midnight when I saw her headlights in the pullout, and I wanted my record to be dead-on accurate.

There had been a whirlwind of stuff happening to me that week, but I didn't put any of it in my record. That was two lifetimes ago. I had been a night watchman at the River Oaks Refinery, a horrible job that I thought I deserved. I was just putting one foot in front of the other. There was a pack of wild dogs in the plant that roved around, nine or ten big dogs, and when I came to every corner, I'd peek around for them. These dogs came out at night and ran the place; every time I saw them or if I heard them, I went the other way. The night I met Baby Grayson and all my life took this turn, those dogs had split up and that's how they got me. I heard them coming up one alley and I ran down the other, where three of the savage animals waited. They weren't German shepherds and they weren't rottweilers or Labradors, but they were some big dogs, all different, up from Mexico I guess, and I was bitten more than twice, but I wasn't eaten alive, which was their intent. I climbed onto the scaffolding above a row of turbines, and I crawled along the catwalk a quarter mile to the guard shack and my old Nissan. I left my badge and my bloody thumbprint on the steel desk and thereby quit.

A half hour later I was almost to the top of Incon Canyon when I saw headlights in the pullout and I stopped to see what it was. There's never a car there. Her Subaru was steaming heavily, and I could see she'd hit a deer even before I walked back and found him twisted on the shoulder, dead. She wouldn't get out of the car, but I talked to her through her window in the dark.

"I'm a night watchman," I yelled, thinking she might feel safe with a member of a security force. I went to show her my badge, but of course it was back at dog hell. "You've smashed your radiator in and you're surely going to burn up your engine!"

"I'm okay," she yelled back. "I'm just going to Rock Creek."

"You won't make it to Rock Creek without burning up your engine!" I said.

"Did I kill that deer?"

"You did," I told her. "Look at your temperature gauge," I said. "You're going to burn this right up. I can give you a ride to Rock Creek if you want! You can get your car tomorrow!"

"It's downhill," she said. "I'm okay. He jumped right out of nowhere! Thanks for stopping!" And she pulled back onto the winding two-lane and started down for Rock Creek, which was nineteen miles.

It's dark at the top of Incon at midnight. The stars come down and rattle the sky real good and you can hear the river working, but it is a lonely place. I didn't need any more lonely places. My leg was throbbing and I felt a new place on the back of my thigh burning. My trousers were about used up. After a minute I went back to the little buck and pulled him well off the road. My prayer was stupid like everything else I was doing those days. I said, "I'm sorry about what happened to you. Good-bye."

When I was in the Nissan, I found myself turning around and heading back down toward Rock Creek. Either I would get rabies and perish in this desolate place or I would come across that woman in the burning Subaru.

I found her about six miles down, and when I pulled up behind the rusted vehicle, she got out of the car and met me halfway. She was wearing a red vest with a name tag on it and black trousers; it was her casino work clothes. "It's me," I said. "Did it seize up and die?"

In the dark I saw her put something in her pocketbook, which though I didn't exactly see it I was sure was a handgun.

"I do need a ride after all," she said. "That car won't go any further tonight."

And so, in the September 5 entry, I describe my giving Baby Grayson a ride down to the shabby cabin at Rock Creek where I met Leo Rosemont, the other principal in my record. By the time we got down there and followed the little two-track through the dark aspen grove to their place against the river, my two legs were both beating hot pain. It was forty miles back to the hospital, and I thought this might just be it for me. I'd drop this nervous woman off at her little forest hovel and pass out somewhere down canyon. I could feel the beads of sweat burning along my hairline already; those dogs had got me good, twisting their big bad teeth in my ass.

Baby and Leo's place was a mean little shed about to slump into the river, and there wasn't a light on when we pulled up in the weedy yard. The starlight off the tin roof and the flashing river lit the whole place a spooky black and white. Baby got out of the car and told me to wait a second while she went in and turned on the lights. Her husband was probably asleep, she said. "Leo," she called. "Leo!"

Baby disappeared into the dark shelter. My wounds were beating against my bones as I waited in the car, and then I heard the brush behind me, and a voice said, "How's it going, Bob?" A figure was standing by the rear tire.

I recoiled and struggled from my vehicle into the fresh dark. I saw light fill the little square windows of the house as I stood. Before I could greet this man or shake his hand or even say my real name, the pain rose up my legs, broke over me, and I went down.

I didn't put that night in the record, how Leo Rosemont hauled me into their hovel and cut my pants off me and scoured the five holes that had been torn in me by the giant dogs from hell with hydrogen peroxide and Betadine and rubbing alcohol as well as great splashes of domestic vodka.

There was a lot I didn't put into my notebook as it thickened, but I recalled it all, even the smells, the way the grit felt on my cheek when I woke on the floor that next dawn.

Every day at the El Sol when I finished what I could of my writing, I blew the brown ink dry and hid the notebook by clipping it to a hanger inside my watchman jacket in the closet. I went outside and stood in the sun for a moment before walking down to the Blue Door. I was grateful for the sun and that one moment when it pressed against my face for another day. I was riven with regrets, and I actively hurt with my love for Baby, but I was going forward with my plan. And the record, though it wouldn't make me eligible for any citizenship awards, would be a true thing, not screwed sideways like everything else I touched, everything so far.

What Mr. Cuppertino liked about *The Price Is Right* was the "Showcase Showdown," where the two contestants bid on their own bevy of prizes. "Oh, for God's sake!" Mr. Cuppertino would cry when the little woman would say $12,500 for the bedroom set, the two motor scooters, and the trip to Orlando. "It's fifteen," he'd say. "Nothing is ever twelve. You can't get a dinette and floor wax for twelve!" And Mr. Cuppertino was always right. He was full of wisdom for that show. I liked watching it with him in the sunny room. The people on the program were always jumping up and down and screaming and clapping both hands over their mouths as they thought of their bids. Every time Roberta Gilstrand would appear standing beside one of the red motor scooters or running her hand along the side of a new car, Mr. Cuppertino would say, "There she is." He told me that if he were my age, he'd write for tickets and go down to Los Angeles and court that gal with every bone in his body. "I wouldn't waste my life up here in Globe with a crazy geezer like me watching TV!"

I found that walking a little bit helped keep the shadows in my mind from closing in, and so in the afternoons when I couldn't sleep, I walked the town and thought about Baby Grayson, whom I had loved desperately a few desperate weeks before. The days in Globe were warm in October, and I walked to the top of Solomon Hill and looked over the dusty mining town as it spilled out below me. My thoughts on these walks were not orderly the way I was laying down the events in the book, but they came in a mess, moments with Baby that did not wait for an invitation to appear, they just crashed through, things she said, things she did.

I was at their cabin for three days laid up with my dog bites, two of which I should have had stitched up, it turns out. Leo Rosemont gave me huge capsules, which I took with short shots of Ten High bourbon whiskey. He had a variety of chemical substances. Baby Grayson folded some blankets on the floor under the one window into a makeshift bed, and that was the name of that tune. You fall in love with your nurse, believe me. I was ripe for it anyway, being against rock bottom and all bit up and feverish, and then Baby bending to me with crackers and soup every time I was awake. She was short and fleshy with the sweetest face on earth. Even with Leo Rosemont in the room (and I already knew he was bad news folded double), I gave myself over to my feelings and with my every expression I presented those feelings to her.

In the afternoon Baby Grayson would change into her work clothes, buttoning her blouse as she walked through the room, and go off in my Nissan to the River of Gold Casino up over Incon Pass. She was a dealer. Standing in the cabin, snapping her chewing gum and pinning on her name tag, she'd say, "I pay the rent."

It was hard to believe rent on such a place could be much. There are a lot of versions of the end of the road, and this was a bad one, a lonely tumbledown two years from falling off the eroding cutbank into the actual river. There was no sound except for the wind in the pines and the rush of the river. I could hear conversations in that garbled friction, voices working all night long. I also could hear Leo Rosemont and Baby in the little bedroom every night and then again in the gray mornings as they huffed and slapped. Her voice was full of alarm and resignation to me where I lay under the chilly window with my clustered wounds burning.

The third day, when I could finally sit up, though I could only just perch on the edge of the chair, Leo Rosemont and I had a talk. It was September 8, and I wrote the interchange in my journal or record, whatever it was. The only table in their place was an old wooden cable spool covered with spills and candle wax and about a dozen golden salt and pepper shakers saying *River of Gold* on them and a giant Tabasco bottle, gummed up and half full, and a yellow plastic flashlight with grease prints on it, and three glass *River of Gold* ashtrays, which brimmed with butts, and Leo Rosemont's bottle of Ten High, which had about an inch left in it. This was a rough-hewn table where you had to be careful where you put your coffee because there were four or five holes in the thing where stuff would drop through.

"Well," Leo said to me as he poured a lick of whiskey into his cold coffee and handed the bottle to me. "You may survive after all."

"I appreciate your help," I told him. I'd sized him up from my nest on the floor, and Leo Rosemont was about six-one and he would have run about one-eighty. His hair was a shiny black and he always had a four-day beard, like some kind of stain. There were blue shadows under his eyes that made him look serious and tired, and he spoke as slowly as anyone I've ever met.

"Glad to be of service," he said. "Those were some worthy dog bites you suffered."

I went ahead and put some whiskey in my coffee.

"You saved Baby with a ride and we were able to assist you," he said. "That's fair right there."

"It is," I said. I was sitting wrapped in the rough blanket.

"We could do one more turn that way," he said. "If you've got a couple weeks."

"I'm unemployed," I told him. "But I'm going to need to get a pair of pants."

It was that day that Leo Rosemont laid out the little plan he'd cooked up. He showed me a stack of black and gold casino chips and asked me what it was. I told him it looked like a stack of ten one-dollar chips from the River of Gold Casino. He told me to look close. I did. It was a stack of the things. Then he smiled and lifted it, and what came up in his hand was a perfect hand-crafted, hand-painted aluminum tube that had covered what remained: a stack of the black and white twenty-five-dollar chips. "If it fooled you," he said, "this thing is good to go."

They did need me for it, which gave me the strangest feeling I'd had in a long time, and I didn't put the feeling in the record, and maybe I should have, because it was a good and powerful feeling. I was part of something. They needed me, and on that far side of the pernicious events to follow, it didn't feel like anything too bad, just a kind of windfall that would keep me in proximity with Baby Grayson, my new angel. After midnight, early on the morning of September 9 of this year, when Baby came home from work, we sat around that nasty round table and went over the details. I put those details, every one, in my written chronicle.

In Globe I began helping Mr. Cuppertino with the motel. It started with me getting up from time to time to register the guests and take their money. At the El Sol almost everyone paid in cash. On Wednesdays I turned the Dumpster so it could be accessed from the alley. And every other day or so I'd sweep or clean the windows in the office and stack the magazines. I was about halfway through my work inscribing my journal, just past the part when I began taking money out of the casino. I would finish the whole thing in two weeks. Then I'd have to make some big decisions.

Mr. Cuppertino hated people on *The Price Is Right* who would bid just one dollar over the last guy. It struck him as being unfair, and he had written a letter to the show about the practice, urging them to adopt a fifty-dollar margin. In response they had sent him two tickets to the show, which he had pinned to the office bulletin board. Whenever we were watching the program and someone pulled the one-dollar stunt, he would shake his head and say, "That snake!" even if it was a woman.

During commercials he'd ask me about myself, the same questions every day. Why isn't a young guy like me married? Isn't my family worried about me? What line of work was I in? Didn't I think Roberta Gilstrand was the most beautiful woman in the world?

He wanted to know if I was in some kind of trouble or needed some help. We'd become friends, kind of, and I agreed with his view about those assholes on *The Price Is Right* who bid a dollar over the last guy, and Mr. Cuppertino kind of wore me down. Every morning I was writing the miserable things I'd done with Baby and Leo, and then I'd end up sitting in his office watching the people on television jump up and down, which was just a pure pleasure akin to solace certainly, and I began to tell him things. I had a faint feeling that he would be the one who finally would turn me in and end my life with eternal jail, but I let things come out bit by bit.

I told him I fell in love with a woman and was nursing my broken heart. This was true. I told him I didn't know what had become of her. This was true. But I feared the worst.

True. It had been an unfortunate triangle involving a guy who was cruel and unscrupulous. This was understated but true. I told him a good deal of my troubles were my fault. True. I told him I was staying on a couple more weeks just to gather my wits. This was essentially true.

Mr. Cuppertino asked me if I was afraid.

I asked him did I act like I was afraid.

He said I did, and I told him I was. This was true, and it was a relief to express, but it didn't diminish the fear that was my steady companion.

At night in Unit 7 of the El Sol in Globe, I lay in bed like one gigantic ear, every bump and scrape starting my heart. Every footstep was Leo Rosemont shuffling up to break down my door, say I told you so, and shoot me dead. When you live on the blade of your fear for weeks, you start to think that you can't wait for the enemy to be made real. I would have welcomed Leo Rosemont into the room any of those nights, but to make his phantom go away forever.

What we had done, of course, is cheat. A casino is a little house of money and Leo's plan was to bleed some of that off. Leo, himself, had already been banned from the casino. They got me some clothes from the St. Vincent store in Incon, a kind of cowboy outfit including a fairly decent Stetson, black, and just about the right size. "When we're all long gone," Leo Rosemont told me, "they'll be talking about some guy in a black hat. A handsome dude who must have charmed little Baby out of her panties and then out of her little mind. That sweet girl would have never crossed the line otherwise." Then he laughed and we started in.

Baby and I would drive up to Incon every afternoon for her shift at the casino. She let me off half a mile away, behind the Incon Gas and Go, for the first time on September 13 at ten minutes to three o'clock. It was our pattern and I put it in my book. I did not put in there about how I felt about my days alone with her, how the very first time we drove away from their evil hovel with me dressed up like Tex from Texarkana, I was lit and floating in unspeakable joy. My heart rattled, but I closed my teeth against it. We had a thirty-minute drive in the lonesome canyon, which to me was a vivid roaring backdrop for my love. I rode in silence, trusting time to reveal to Baby Grayson how I adored her and what that might mean.

I was mightily relieved to be away from the dark, smoky cabin and the greasy personage of Leo Rosemont, whose major activity was to sip whiskey while he talked about what he'd do to each of his former bosses on the various road crews and logging crews and at the telemarketing group and two restaurants where he'd worked. He'd already done some of it and was proud of vandalizing their private property, their lunches and cars, and the clever way he'd harassed them via telephone, scaring the wives and children of these men. I was scared of Leo Rosemont from the get-go.

At four P.M. every night for the rest of September, including Saturdays and Sundays, after having a coffee and factory-made Danish inside the Gas and Go, I walked from behind that solitary building through the dusty, litter-blasted sage toward the lights of the River of Gold Casino.

My pattern was the same each of the twenty days, and it never varied, even the night that Baby finally came to understand my feelings for her and we stopped off the shoulder at the top of Incon Canyon on the way back to the river cabin, the very gravel spur where we first met, and in that dark place she showed me the love that seemed my very destiny. In the casino my pattern was simply to stop by the roulette table and see Baby, and if the pit boss was down by the craps table, she would palm Leo Rosemont's aluminum sleeve over a stack of twenty-five-dollar chips and slide it to me in return for my twenty-dollar bill. I'd play the ten one-dollar chips right up and put the fake stack in my pocket. If the pit boss was up behind her, I'd play ten and leave, stopping by three hours later during her second shift. Every night with this simple plan, I pocketed exactly $250 in the black and gold chips. I stuffed the chips, still in their tube, into the front pocket of my pants, and I delivered them to Leo Rosemont every night at midnight when we got back. I was not to cash any of the chips.

When I had my score, I was to depart the casino, and I did, taking a tall Coke in a plastic cup from the waitress station adjacent the bar, and I walked into the lonely night.

This was the strangest job I ever had, but I walked out into the dark with my pockets bulging and the knowledge that at eleven Baby would pull the Nissan behind the Gas and Go and find me sitting back there on a dairy crate and we would head for home, such as it was.

Mr. Cuppertino liked Plinko. About once a week contestants on *The Price Is Right* would get to play Plinko, where they earn the big Plinko chips by guessing the digits in the prices of spray starch and wheat nuggets, and then they drop the chips into the huge Plinko board and the chips bounce down toward the money slots. It was fun to watch the way the discs pinged off the nails, hopping from side to side, slowly working toward the ten-thousand-dollar slot or the one-hundred-dollar slot. Roberta Gilstrand stood below in pink Capri pants with her graceful hands on her hips. "They got the thing fixed just about right," Mr. Cuppertino said. "It's a fair go. That ten thousand is a long shot, but it happens. I've seen it happen."

He'd advise the players about where to drop their chips, saying, "Left, dear, left, to the left, further left," but the people always dropped them down the middle, time after time. We rooted for the Plinko players, but then we rooted for everybody except the people who bid one dollar over the last guy. We were watching a young sailor drop the Plinko chips one morning when Mr. Cuppertino asked me if I would help him with a little project. He was going to refurbish the twelve units of the El Sol, and he needed someone to drive a truck to Hotel Surplus in Phoenix and back.

It was a big yellow truck with a twelve-foot box, certainly the biggest truck I'd driven, and Mr. Cuppertino was gleeful because the whole deal only cost him nineteen dollars for the day. He'd been happy since he'd taped the cardboard sign to the locked office door: BACK AT 3. "God, I love a road trip!" he said as we wound through the rocky canyons and down onto the desert floor and the hazy unending metropolis of Phoenix in the flat noon light. "It's good for a person to get out. Mickey knew that. We drove all over the Midwest; her folks lived in Fort Wayne. That's way up there. You can't bury yourself in an office and hand out keys your whole life."

The larger world seen from the elevated cab seemed big and bright to me, too. Sleeping on the damp floor of the river cabin had not made me an optimist, but now with my written record almost done, and the sunshine crashing down everywhere, I felt almost well.

I had everything written down except the final week. That week, just as we'd done for the two previous, Baby Grayson and I went to the River of Gold Casino every night, and we used Leo Rosemont's aluminum sleeve like a perfect tool and took ten twenty-five-dollar chips from the casino. On the tenth night, I broke my silence with Baby and asked her how she felt about all of this. We were headed for home, rising off the flat toward the summit, and she said, "About what?"

"Taking this money. Leo. Me."

"I like it," she said. "If we're careful, we'll get new lives out of this." It was something Leo had told us.

"What do you want in a new life?" I asked her.

"I don't know. A new life."

"What about me?" I asked her. I had started talking and it was easy to cross the line. "How do you feel about me?"

"Pretty good," she said. "You're doing good."

"Do you love Leo?" I asked her.

She guided us through the three switchbacks at the top. "Sure," she said. "Why not?"

"He's not always real good to you," I said. "Is he?"

"I don't know," she said. "He's okay."

I couldn't read what was going on, but my heart was beating. "Look," I said. "Pull over at the top and I'll check the radiator."

She did that and I stepped out into the canyon dark. You could hear the river, and the car ticked as I went around the front. I didn't even open the hood, but I went right around to Baby's door and I opened it so she could get out.

"What is it, Eugene?" she said to me.

The truth that had been waiting for ten days burst from me. "I want you." I pulled her up and kissed her soft face. Her body against me was beyond imagining.

"What do you want?" she asked, genuinely confused. But she was kissing me back and her fleshy arms were around my back. We squirmed against the car like that for two or three minutes, as far as you go with clothes, and I became certain I had her cooperation. "We can do this," she said to me. "If you want to." She started draping her clothing over the trunk of my Nissan. "No problem," she said. "Come on." And she directed me through the rest of our roadside session with a fervor that I savored as much as her warm body under mine.

Twenty minutes later in the car, I straightened her hair with my fingers as she drove and she flinched, saying, "What are you doing?"

"Just fixing your hair," I said. "I don't want Leo to know."

She looked at me, sweetly, blankly, and her expression scared me. "Okay," she said. "Whatever."

"No," I said. "Leo mustn't find out. Don't let Leo know what happened."

"Okay by me," she said, and then she braked there for Rock Creek and turned off the hardtop into the forest and the trail that led to the dark cabin.

That night, as always, Leo took the stack of chips from the aluminum sleeve and looked at it and smiled. Then he held the sleeve in the short glow of the candle and examined it slowly, and then he'd say the number of days left. He always said the number of days left, and the night that Baby first gave herself fully to me there on the summit turnout, he said, Nine days to go. Some nights then he'd offer me a little Ten High and some nights he'd just start in repairing the aluminum sleeve, using his magnifying glass and his penknife and the small jars of model-airplane enamel. I watched Baby hang her vest on the chair and unbutton her blouse going into their bedroom, and the door swung back till it was half closed.

"You meeting any people over there at the River of Gold?" he asked me.

"Nobody."

"Bartender? Cocktail waitress?"

"Like you told me," I said, "I don't talk to them, and I don't sit at the bar."

"How many words do you say between leaving and coming back?"

"I don't know," I said.

"Guess," he said.

"Two hundred," I said.

He thought a minute, then looked up from re-scribing edges in our device. "You get coffee at the Gas and Go."

"Yes," I said.

"That kid is going to remember you."

"No more coffee," I said.

"That's a better plan," he said. He set the hollow cylinder down. "You talk to Baby?"

"Some," I said. "I tell her it went all right when she picks me up."

"Good," he said, palming the chips stack by stack. "You know my name?"

"Leo," I said.

"My last name."

"I don't know it," I told him. He looked me over and said again, "Good. You still headed west when we're done?" I had told him I was going to take my share and go west.

"Yes I am."

"Good deal, my man. Nine more days and you'll be off to your new life, whatever."

I slept poorly in the river cabin. My legs ached at night and I listened for Leo and Baby, and every night the noises came. I knew with certainty that Leo would kill me if he found out about Baby and me, and that thought kept the sleep off me. I had made a mistake, but instead of wanting to retract it, like every other sad turn I'd taken, I wanted to push this one through, keep it up, take Baby with me to a new life. I could see us happy. We'd be good together, but the clock was ticking over my head. At that point, I had fewer than nine days.

The Hotel Surplus Depot was two connected warehouses on a railroad siding on the west side of Phoenix, and there were great stacks of furniture inside, heaped like kids had done it. All the couches stood on end and the end tables themselves were piled up like boxes. There were two long rows of framed seascapes on the floor, the sun setting in every one. It was pretty interesting, all that used stuff. I'd never seen a mountain of a thousand lamps before. A handful or so other shoppers poked through, working in teams toward the dresser or shelving that wasn't scratched too badly, and that's finally what Mr. Cuppertino and I did, selecting a dozen nice walnut-paneled bedside tables and a dozen chairs padded with a blue fabric and as many heavy-duty towel bars. These were heavy chrome affairs with a kind of rack shelf. Mr. Cuppertino was lit up by these bargains. I mean, the chairs were six dollars each and the racks four. He was really tickled to find twelve relatively decent cover quilts in a blue floral pattern for three bucks each. I had to agree with him when he said, as we loaded the truck, "We done good. We pillaged this place. Those towel racks would list for forty bucks on *The Price Is Right!* They are known as the Waldorf Towel Caddie and they are not cheap."

It was a good feeling driving back with that big load of treasures. Mr. Cuppertino told me how he and his wife, Mickey, had done this in smaller vehicles over the years, waiting for a call from the manager of the Holiday Inn in Apache Junction and then going down for his leftovers. The Hotel Surplus Depot had only been going for about fifteen years, and it made things a lot easier. "We'll do the carpet next spring," he told me. "If you want to stay around."

Well, I'd been thinking about it. Those towel racks weren't going to put themselves up, and Mr. Cuppertino told me he had a good power drill for the job. What I was thinking was: I'd like to put something on the wall and have it stay for a few years.

It's funny about writing things down. I was working in my notebook every morning, trying to get the bare bones of my times with Baby and Leo in there, just the facts, something the proper authorities could use. But I couldn't do that. The way it works is that it's never just the facts. I'd write down the fundamentals, but when I came to the night that Baby had dirtied the bottom of her feet by standing naked with me against the warm side of my Nissan, it all changed. I'd go on a little bit. You're writing in the predawn dark and you go on a little bit. I put in there about the way she'd slow down at the summit every night after our first night and look over at me in the dark and I'd nod and we'd go at it without a word, except maybe a hurried "Here," or words meant only to indicate we were still breathing, like "Okay" and "Well." Every night we stopped there in the thinner air and she mostly led the way, and I wrote in the journal that she led the way—and more than one way. She put her hand on my hip and on the back of my neck with an affectionate familiarity. This was every night with the clock ticking on our dubious enterprise, and I became joyously convinced that Baby loved me, for she came at me with an ardor I'd never known, and she held nothing back. One night, and I don't recall which it was in that crazy week, she looked at me from where I had her on the tailgate of my vehicle and she said, "You like this, don't you." It wasn't a question, but I answered it anyway and said that yes I did.

It was after the third night when we were back in the car straightening our clothes as she drove down the canyon toward Rock Creek that I asked her Leo's last name and she told me Rosemont without hesitating and I knew our collusion was complete. She told me that she had met him at the River of Gold Casino last spring. He had been nice to her—courtly, she said—and they started to date. She didn't know he was living in his car after his release from Medium, which is what they call Incon Medium Security Prison. He'd been in there two years for being part owner of a meth lab somewhere in the hard desert outside of Gallup, and in prison he had learned fine arts and crafts, carving wood, and working with some jewelry. It was in Medium that he got the idea for our aluminum sleeve.

Right away he'd gotten into some trouble in the casino, was barred from it, because of a dispute over a slot machine.

A woman claimed he had distracted her with a story about her car in the parking lot and he had taken her place and her 640 credits on the Dollar Diamond Three Way slot machine she'd been playing. The security video showed she was right, and he was forbidden from the place. That had been almost three weeks before I had my ass chewed up by the wild refinery hounds and drove Baby home that fateful night.

I put this story in the record even though I had it second-hand from Baby, and I put in the last four nights, including all the rough stuff I heard and saw before I went back to the cabin one last time and then slipped away through the trees and hitchhiked down Incon Canyon to Red Post and took a bus here to Globe and the El Sol Motel. I finished with the date of October 4 and the name of this motel, the El Sol, and the name of Mr. Cuppertino, my new friend. My notebook was fat as a Bible, swollen with all the inky pages, so that I had to close it with a rubber band. I signed the story as I had written it, and I clothespinned it to the hanger and put the hanger in the jacket in my closet, and I zipped the jacket up, and I was done with it.

There were various games that repeated on *The Price Is Right*—Bulls-Eye, Clock, Poker, Push Over, Groceries, One Away (where each digit in the price of the car is one away from the real number)—and while Plinko was Mr. Cuppertino's favorite, he watched Groceries with real attention. He commented on all the products. "You ever had that toaster pizza?" he'd ask me.

"I haven't," I'd tell him.

"Let's pick some up later and give it a try. Mickey would not approve, but this is my new life we're talking about."

We agreed that we neither one of us wanted to win a year's supply of spray-on sizing, which they gave away freely in any week, and Mr. Cuppertino swore aloud when they offered the jumbo bottle of Lightning-Rooter, which you pour in your drains to unclog them and which evidently had caused the motel some harm in years past. He liked the bakery goods, especially Aunt Dorothy brand this and thats, but he had no use for hair spray or the knickknacks like vases or picture frames or the set of miniature clocks that turned out to be worth nine hundred dollars.

"I'd like to go out there," he told me. On the screen, they were showing the address to send away for tickets. "I've already got those two tickets."

"To the show?"

"Right. That'd be a road trip. We'll close up for a week or get George up from the Blue Door to run the place. I'd like to see Miss Roberta Gilstrand in person and get Bob's autograph." He looked over at me, then he scanned the upper corners of the office, all four. "We're going to have to paint this place this winter. The latex they put out is about a four-year paint anymore." He wove his fingers together. "This place about wears me out. You want a job?"

It was a good thing to hear, but then something happened that stopped my heart and made the world go slow motion. It was my old car. My Nissan turned in off Durrant Street and pulled to a stop under the El Sol's office canopy. I felt a voltage bring me to my feet, and without a word to Mr. Cuppertino, I slipped past him and the counter, through the curtained door into his private quarters, where I had never before ventured. I stood in his dark little living room, leaning against the wall, listening to the voices from the office: Bob Barker on *The Price Is Right*, Mr. Cuppertino doing business, and then, another voice that I knew very well, Leo Rosemont.

A moment later Mr. Cuppertino stepped back and went past me to his stove for the coffeepot. Bringing it back, he said to me, "That's the guy, isn't it?"

"Yes," I told him.

"Well, that's a stroke of luck," he said. "He's checked in to number ten, and he says he's looking for a fella owes him money. Medium build, short dark hair, name of Eugene, doesn't know the last name. The guy may have a black cowboy hat."

"I'm sure that man intends to kill me."

"Because of that girl," Mr. Cuppertino said.

"Because of the girl and that I took a packet of money from him."

"Those are reasons," he said to me. "Those are good ones." My heart was driving me into my chair deeper and deeper. Mr. Cuppertino put a spoon of sugar in my coffee, which he knows I like, and we sat in his crowded parlor, and he talked to the contestants all through the "Showcase Showdown" while my mind raced, stalled, and spiraled.

The last time I'd seen Leo Rosemont, he'd been mad. In the morning dark at the cabin, I heard the two of them struggling in their bed. Baby was noisy in a struggle and I knew the rhythm of her cries very well, but that last day it was different, broken and odd, and I understood that he was hurting her. Suddenly the sounds stopped and I heard Leo's footsteps. With my eyes closed tight, I felt his rough bare foot on my face. "Hey, boy." He rocked his foot. "Let's have a meeting." I opened my eyes and said, "What?" but he kept his foot hard against the side of my head. He was naked. "The truth has come out, and your ass is grass." With that he gave me a little kick, shoving off. I sat up and he returned in a pair of Levi's. He sat at the splintered table and lit a cigarette. "You're fired," he said. "Did you think Baby wouldn't tell me?" He blew a tremendous column of smoke at the ceiling, a gray plume in the raw light. "It never works with three, that I've seen. Three just don't work." Baby padded to the doorway wearing only her white work shirt, and she crossed to Leo and sat on his lap with her head tucked up under his. "It works with two mostly and with four, but not three. You think you want her, that she'd be better off with you, away from the likes of me. You could take care of her. You're only about half dumb, and you've got a bad case on this cutie, right? And me, I think she's mine, of course, boy, because she is. She's exactly the kind of woman who needs to stay away from the likes of you. You, my friend, are a sinking stone. You're sunk here."

Leo leaned forward and crushed his cigarette onto the rough plank, and I saw Baby cling tighter. "But I'm not going to kill you, so that's the good news. But you've lost your share and you've lost your car and you got to get off the property in the next five minutes, and if I ever see you again, I will hurt you." He pointed his long dirty finger at me and I stared at it, past it, at the side of Baby's streaked face, but she did not turn.

I squirmed into my clothes and tied my shoes tight, and I stuffed the black cowboy hat on my head. I stood and said good-bye, but neither of them replied. So I dropped out of the front door and hurried down the lane as if headed for the canyon road.

Three hours later I heard the Nissan growling along the dirt lane, and I saw it bump away toward the canyon highway. Her days of driving to work were over. I lay in the leaves all that time. When it grew quiet again and I could only hear the river and the voices in it, I walked back to the terrible cabin, and on my hands and knees, I fished all the black and gold casino chips from the center hollow of the wooden spool table where Leo Rosemont had stashed them. He should have considered my point of view as I lay on the floor every night. It was no wonder with Leo and Baby raising a lusty racket that my eyes stayed open, and that from that vantage I spied the edge of one of the chips where it lodged in that cracked wooden cylinder. I stuffed newspapers into the space and covered just the top with a scattering of chips; he wouldn't find them gone until he and Baby cashed out. I shouldered my little day pack full of my clothes, such as they were, and about a pound of casino chips—$5,100—and I hit the highway and hitched west.

At the El Sol, I spent the whole morning in a sour sweat hiding out in Mr. Cuppertino's apartment. At noon he told me that Leo Rosemont had finally gone out, probably to find some lunch, and so I slipped down to my room. I was at the curtains every ten minutes, but my car did not return. Finally I lay on my bed and my thoughts lay upon me like cold stones.

After nine P.M., Mr. Cuppertino came in with a white paper bag of sandwiches in one hand and something in his other that I recognized: my spiral notebook. He put them both on the kitchenette table and spread the food onto two napkins under the hanging lamp: pastrami sandwiches, dill pickles, and two paper cups of coffee with sugar packets. Mr. Cuppertino sat down and touched his fingertips together. "Let's eat something," he said. His eyes were bright, tired. I went to the window and peeked out yet again, and this time I saw my Nissan right in front of my room. "Oh my God."

"It's your car," he said. "Isn't it? It's in the story as your car. I got it back."

I sat with him. "What?"

He tapped the thick notebook in which I had written what I had written. "I'm sorry. It's not my custom to go into a guest's room, but in this case I needed to be sure about what I was going to do."

I was sitting down again, dislocated, my heart lifting at my shoulders and neck. "I've made ten mistakes, big ones," I said. "I had a sore love for the woman involved. It was the wrong thing."

Mr. Cuppertino closed his hands like a book and delivered me a long hard look. "Well, my friend, this has been a good month for me in a dismal year as shitty as I've known. I told you that Mickey's death was bad news, but you should have seen the seven months before. She was an angel and she died, so I figure what I just did to reclaim your vehicle ranks as real small change." He leaned back and pulled his old pistol from his pocket and placed it on my notebook. "When you walked up to the old El Sol a month ago, Joey Cuppertino was about giving it up." He worked his fingers against his closed eyes and went on. "I started to figure you might want to stay on. We could paint this place and plan our trip out to California. That'd be good for both of us." He lifted half of his sandwich and tipped it once at me before taking a bite. "You could move into Unit 12 at the end with the big kitchen. Old Globe is dusty and dry but, Eugene, there's worse."

So we painted our way through the old El Sol, unit by unit. We started every day right after *The Price Is Right.* "You know what the toughest item in a showcase is?" he asked me.

"A boat," I said. "I've seen some big-money boats."

"A trip," he said. "Seven days in Egypt; that could be anything."

When I told him I was not going to jump up and down and act like an idiot, he told me to relax. "If we jump, we jump." He's right. You can't really tell how you'll react until you get there.